The Last Cabin

Other Books By Mike Lein
The "Life at the Cabin" Series

FIREWOOD HAPPENS
Life, Liberty, and the Pursuit of Happiness in Minnesota's Northwoods.
A simple book about the simple life at a simple cabin in the Northwoods. Winner of the Midwest Independent Publishers Association 2016 Award for Humor.

DOWN AT THE DOCK
More Stories of the Good Life in the Northwoods.
Life at the cabin gets more complicated. A look at serious subjects such as Big Foot, skinny-dipping, and possible firewood theft. Winner of the Midwest Independent Publishers Association 2017 Award for Humor.

THE CROOKED LAKE CHRONICLES
Mostly True Stories of Life Up North.
Lightly embellished tales of the things that happen, the people you meet, and the struggles with Mother Nature that occur when you enjoy the simple life in the Great Outdoors. Finalist for the Midwest Independent Publishers Association 2019 Award for Humor.

CABIN FEVER
Life Goes on in the Northwoods.
What's an outdoor writer to do when he's stuck

inside during a pandemic? Write a book about life at the cabin and other outdoor adventures to fight off a bad case of cabin fever. Winner of the Midwest Independent Publishers Association 2022 Award for Humor.

FOR THE HUNTER:
HUNTING AROUND
Adventures of a Hunter in The Great Outdoors.
A mix of adventures, free advice, and lessons learned by a hunter roaming wild places with good dogs and good friends.

Notes and Acknowledgments

The Last Cabin is the sixth book I've written, so I've had previous experience in writing these "Notes and Acknowledgments." And it's getting easier with every book because the same great people were involved along the way.

Writing a book is one thing. Publishing a book is a whole other animal. It's a challenge to publish a well-edited book that people will buy, read, enjoy, and recommend to their friends. I've been lucky that my previous five books seem to have met those qualifications and not just because of my "skills" as a writer.

The Jackpine Writers' Bloc has published all these books. I may sound like a broken record, having acknowledged this organization in the previous five. But this truth bears repeating, as does the fact that the organization is not a faceless private company or corporation. It's people like Sharon Harris and Tarah Wolff who edit my bad grammar and lousy punctuation, and then do all the electronic wizardry needed to publish a book in this digital age.

Even before all that comes the work of the dedicated members of the writers' group hosted by the Jackpine Writers' Bloc. These fellow seasoned writers suffer through drafts of my stories, make constructive comments, and keep me learning about things like punctuation and grammar. Hopefully I return this big favor by offering constructive comments on their work.

Not to be lost in this process is the illustrator. Erik Espeland of Erik Espeland Art and Illustration provides the cover art and chapter sketches. Many people do judge a book by its cover. Erik makes sure the cover catches these people's eyes and makes them take the next step of picking up the book. Check him and his work out. He is, as I call him, "a Real Artist."

I always ask friends and family for ideas for book titles, especially for the subtitle. It should be no surprise that most of these suggestions end up not being suitable for publication. Especially the ones suggested by the characters that end up being featured in the stories. In this case my favorite unused one was suggested by the oldest son, Andy— *The Last Cabin*—"Blood, Sweat and Beers."

That one does fit in some ways as much of this book revolves around the building of the big fancy addition to our original humble cabin. The addition is big by my standards and fancy in that it has indoor plumbing, at least for the ladies. And the work so far has involved blood, sweat, and beers. Thankfully the blood that was shed was mine and not that of the many friends, neighbors, family, and a few skilled tradesmen who assisted in the project.

But anyway, my sweaty hat is off to all those that helped. I owe you a few more beers and hopefully no more blood of mine or yours is shed as the building project and other adventures continue. Because a cabin is never really finished, and neither are adventures.

An edited version of "A Change in Power" was published in *Talking Stick 30*, an anthology published yearly by The Jackpine Writers' Bloc, Inc.

Edited versions of "Snow" and "Standards" were published in *Talking Stick 31*, an anthology published yearly by The Jackpine Writers' Bloc, Inc.

"Off My Grid" by Jim Lein was originally published in *Colorado Serenity Magazine*.

The author's son Steve Lein contributed to "A Change in Power."

Table of Contents

The Last Cabin

FOREWORD
IN THE BEGINNING

When people ask which of my books is my favorite, I always turn the question back on them. "So, do you want me to pick my favorite child while I'm at it?"

That usually gets a laugh, and we move on to discussing the books. I also tell them that the books don't have to be read in the order in which they were published. Hopefully they all stand alone. But I always recommend they start with the first— *Firewood Happens*—"Life, Liberty, and the Pursuit of Happiness in Minnesota's Northwoods." It has received many good reviews within the trade, won the Midwest Independent Publishers Association's award for "Humor," and most of all, has sold thousands of copies and continues to sell years after the publication date.

I call *Firewood Happens* "a simple book about the simple life." Or "uncomplicated and innocent." But as we know, life goes on and things get more complicated. That's the premise of *The Last Cabin*. We have some adventures and make some progress as life goes on and gets more complicated. We enjoy road trips at other cabins in other wild places. We move on from our simple little non-complicated cabin, with electricity but no running water and a wood stove, into the bigger more complicated world of indoor plumbing, a real kitchen, and space, including bedrooms for family and guests to spread out in.

The complications that will come with all that include heating bills, leaking toilets, broken well and sewer pumps, and guests who may overstay their welcome.

Here's a quick snapshot of history covered in the other books, just in case you stumble upon *The Last Cabin* as your first exposure to my writings about outdoorsy life.

Way back in the last century, my wife Marcie and I decided it was time to find our own slice of Northwoods Paradise. We had attended college in the north country, spent vacations "Up North" at resorts, and enjoyed many quick weekend getaways at friends' cabins. It was time for a place of our own.

After searching the countryside and our souls, looking for that perfect place, we stumbled upon it. Well, it wasn't quite perfect. There were bugs, bears, and some "elevation" as they say in the real estate business. On the other hand, it was on a small quiet lake, on the edge of thousands of acres of state forest and had space and privacy. It was also affordable.

In the first ten years of ownership, we went from summer camping to year-round weekend use in the simple two-room cabin I built with the help of friends and family. Adventures at the cabin were many. The ones I could air in public became the first four of my "Life at the Cabin" books. And since we like to travel to other wild places, some road trip adventures happened too. Life was simple for a few more years. We aged and the family grew as the adventures at the cabin and other outdoorsy wild places continued.

So here we are today, book number five about life at the cabin and other adventures. It might be the final one in the series. But life goes on. So maybe not . . .

DRIVEWAY

Driveway

When you sign the final pile of paperwork to purchase a piece of forest property or the perfect peaceful lake shore, the real work begins. This work may be easier for those disposed towards hiring qualified contractors and doling out checks in exchange for invoices. But for us do-it-yourselfers and/or the financially challenged wanna-be cabin owners, this means grabbing a tool and getting to work acquiring good old-fashioned sweat equity.

First up is access to the property. You can't enjoy what you can't get to, and enjoyment is what you bought it for. Spouses and children are more likely to enjoy the property and make it easier to spend more time and money on further projects, if they can get to the enjoyable features of the property and enjoy them. Thus, an adequate driveway is needed and the sooner the better.

I thought we had a leg up on lots of folks in this group right from the beginning. The property Marcie and I chose to invest in was part of a small development of six large lots. I "discovered" the development before the lots were offered on the open competitive market and made the developer an offer he couldn't refuse. I'd pay full asking price for our chosen lot, no haggling or questions asked, if he

9

agreed to put in a driveway as part of the deal. Since I'm a top-notch negotiator, he agreed to construct a couple of new driveways branching off the existing main access road. All of us property owners would have our own little road system, formally recorded as easements in the property records. It sounded like a good deal at the time. The other neighbors and I could share maintenance costs like gravel and snowplowing. Maybe it would even help to get to know each other and build a sense of community as we worked together to maintain our shared road.

Marcie and I drove north on one fine October day to view the recently installed driveway and make sure the developer had done it right before signing that pile of paperwork. We hit the peak of autumn colors on a perfect sunny day. The maples, oaks, and aspens lining the new path through them had dropped a few leaves and paved the road in gold, orange, and rust, just for us. A ruffed grouse even strutted down the road ahead of the truck as a welcoming committee of one.

The main access road, and our shared driveway branching out from it, had some issues. There was a steep hill as you drove in on the main road. From there, the side road climbed up another steep slope to get to our lot and one other. These hills would surely develop deep rutted washouts when thunderstorms sent rivers of rainwater running down them. Winter's snow and ice would also cause some hair-raising moments as we spun tires up and then slid back down. But this corridor through one thousand feet of forest cleared the way for developing a campsite and a head start on using the site. We went home happy and signed that pile of paperwork.

All of us pioneers in this little community enjoyed some benefits of the shared access road and driveways for a few years. Snowplowing costs less per person when split multiple ways. Likewise, the new gravel needed whenever one of the hills washed out was cheaper when everyone paid up and lent a hand to spread it out. A couple of the other lot owners even decided to build homes and move in year-round. That meant that any storm-downed trees might be chain-sawed and moved off the common part of the road when us weekenders showed up. The year-round neighbors also provided a security system of sorts since any bad guys or snoopers had to navigate the shared road past occupied homes to get to our property.

Now play some ominous music in the background while I narrate in a deep serious voice. Ready? "Mike and Marcie thought they would live happily ever after with their shared driveway and their perfect piece of North Country Paradise. Then the problems began . . ."

Some, I repeat some, of the folks that shared the main driveway didn't always kick in cash for the extra gravel needed when a nasty thunderstorm created a gully down one of the hills. Soon the snowplow guy was pretty unhappy about unpaid bills too. It was also apparent that at least one neighbor had other potential problems. We won't go into those in-depth. However, I can't help but mention one driveway-related episode from a very trying period.

It was midnight in the dead of winter on a dark and stormy night. Honest, I ain't making this up, this time, for the dramatic effect. It was darker than dark, and the wind was blowing snowflakes sideways when I turned off the county road after a long drive north after work. I almost collided with the rear-end of a pickup truck parked just inside the trees, blocking the beginning of the driveway.

That one particular problem neighbor had decided that no one would need the driveway on a dark and stormy night. He could park in the middle of it and walk to his house since he hadn't paid to have his part of the driveway plowed, his old truck had bald tires, and the four-wheel drive was out of commission. He also didn't follow proper North Country courtesy practices and leave the pickup keys on the seat or under the visor just in case someone did show up and needed to move the truck. I know. I looked. I might also mention that he didn't answer his phone when I tried calling. Maybe he hadn't paid that bill either.

I couldn't get around the truck. It was parked smack dab in the middle of the narrowest part of the driveway. Not having a chainsaw handy to widen the driveway, I resigned myself to a cold walk in the middle of a howling blizzard on a dark and stormy night uphill both ways. I put on a warm jacket and boots and trudged through the blowing snow, without a flashlight, some one-thousand feet or more to his house. As I was making this trudge, I was thinking of the many unkind words that I wanted to say to him but probably shouldn't.

The opportunity for those unkind words did not arise. I woke up his dog as I pounded on his front door. This worthless mutt never liked me and now threatened my life and that of my children should I attempt to enter her domain. If the neighbor heard me pounding and yelling or his dog snarling and barking, he chose not to drag himself out of a warm bed and answer the door. I gave up, left the rabid dog behind, and trudged back uphill to my truck through the blizzard on the dark and stormy night. There I warmed up with the heater blowing on "HIGH," considering options and uttering more unkind words.

Hotel for the night? Walk in to my cabin, uphill through the blizzard on a dark and stormy night, leaving the driveway double-blocked and the neighbor mad at ME should he drag himself out of that warm bed and try to get to work early in the morning?

The Last Cabin

I went back to his truck one more time and rooted around in the dark, under seats and floor mats and in the glove box, hoping there was a spare key hidden in the junk-cluttered interior. I finally emptied the ample contents of the center storage consul onto the passenger's seat. There, at the absolute bottom of it, I found a lone key with the truck manufacturer's logo and name. The damn truck started when I used the key.

I moved my truck out onto the road into a perilous position should an early snowplow roar down the county road. I backed the offending truck out and then gave it hell ahead into the snowbank on one side of the driveway. The key was left in the ignition. Maybe someone would steal the rust bucket and solve this problem. I drove on to my own cabin to fire up the wood stove and warm up while continuing to speak unneighborly words about this particular neighbor.

The neighbor never took the time to ask or apologize about this incident in the short time he had remaining as a neighbor. It turns out he wasn't paying the mortgage either.

Sorry about that tirade. Someone had to say it since it represents the ugly side of sharing a driveway with a pack of people.

Things did calm down for a short period after this guy moved on. But they started going downhill again, just like that expensive driveway gravel in a

July thunderstorm. Maintaining those steep hills proved to be problematic. Different materials were tried. Crushed concrete proved to be the best option as far as stability, but certainly not the most cost-effective. The more the driveway got used, as we all spent more time at our own paradises, the more the wear and tear, and expenses, added up.

Now here comes the good part of having neighbors. Some of them do become friends that you share afternoon deck beers, campfires, and pontoon rides with. One of these approached me with an idea. "Mike," he says, "how about we build a new driveway? One that comes in from the county road and just crosses our own land. Make it all legal with recorded easements. Build it the right way without any steep hills. And just deal with each other. You and me. That's all."

He had to overcome some Scandinavian stubbornness and frugality on my part. As I pointed out to him, I had already paid for one perfectly good (well, almost perfect) driveway and over twenty-five years of performing and paying for our share of the maintenance. I was also planning the addition to our cabin and really didn't want to spend some of my limited funds on something I already had. But he prevailed. We came to an agreement over a few of those deck beers and he took charge of the project. He got bids from the county's best road contractor, and from the attorneys and surveyors needed for the legal stuff. He then presented me with a plan that included sweat equity in the driveway. We would fire up our chainsaws and clear the trees off the proposed path ourselves, thus saving big money.

I made the decision to overcome my stubborn frugal genes and listen to common sense. My wife and kids liked the idea too, having become tired of listening to me and my neighbor friend complain about the existing driveway. Now came the sweat equity part of the project.

I usually don't mind some quality time with my chainsaw. It makes me feel like a manly Up North kinda guy, gives me material to write about, and provides cheap heat for the cabin on the nine months' worth of dark and stormy nights that we seem to be experiencing these days. However, I had just spent most of the fall and winter having quality time with my chainsaw. I had stacked up enough firewood for three- or four-years' worth of dark and stormy winter nights because I was planning on working on the cabin addition for three, or four, or ten years. But clearing three football-fields-long worth of new driveway would provide more firewood and save a significant amount of money. I sharpened the chains on that chainsaw and fired it up. Then I had to wait.

Normally I would have preferred to tackle a job like this in the spring or fall when the heat is not so hot, and the bugs are not so buggy. In this case, the road contractor asked us to wait until July to cut the trees down to two-foot-high stumps for his bulldozer to push aside and bury. "The trees help dry the soil as they grow and suck up moisture," he explained. "It makes my job easier, quicker, and cheaper."

Who's gonna argue with that perfect country logic?

We got the required permit for the new access from the county road and waited for early July. The contractor stopped by, gave us the go-ahead, and added some after-the-fact wisdom. "You probably could have started sooner since we are in the middle of a drought."

Off into the woods my neighbor and I went, each with his own plan on how to handle his half of the trees in a timely manner. I figured that burning one tank of chainsaw gas a day, in the cool and less buggy July mornings, would get my share of the job done. My partner figured that ten trees a day, cut and stacked in the early morning hours, would cover his part.

We soon agreed that progress was not progressing fast enough. The day might come when the contractor would show up with his trusty bulldozer and not find a clear path to make into a driveway. We both stepped up our efforts, working longer, fighting more bugs, swearing, and sweating in the middle of a hot summer with little rain, the smoke of distant forest fires hanging thick in the air, mixing with the blue exhaust fumes of our chainsaws.

The effort became a true partnership and a challenge to our reputation as manly Northwoods men. Forget the deer flies, the mosquitoes, the horse flies, the ticks, and the heat. Forget that we would both rather be enjoying those beers on the deck. Should one of us take a break for a deck beer or to cool down in the lake, you could bet the sound of the other's chainsaw would call from the woods, shaming the slacker into putting on another round of bug spray and walking back into the forest with his own chainsaw in hand.

The tree-cutting portion of the project was finished in late July. Some three-hundred-fifty trees were toppled, cut, and stacked off to the side of a stump-filled path through the woods. We survived with all limbs intact, but bug-bitten and dehydrated. It was "sweat equity" in every sense of those words.

The contractor didn't show up as soon as we would have liked. But that's life in the North Country. Things just move along at a slower pace and under relaxed schedules. When he did show up, dirt flew. Some nights the bulldozer's headlights shined and the diesel-fueled engine growled late past sunset and into the early morning, the sights and sounds of a monster devouring the forest. Stumps popped out of the ground and were buried. Dirt

Driveway

moved from hills on the north end to low spots on the south end. Gravel was delivered, spread, and packed.

We were soon strolling down the new curving path through the woods, enjoying a beer and tossing balls for the dogs. All without worrying about traffic from other neighbors or who was going to pay to fix the next pothole or rut. As an added benefit, the project's costs came in well below budget due to the contractor's expertise and my neighbor's project management skills. I had to wonder why "we" hadn't done this years before . . .

Given all that, here's some words of wisdom for those that might be thinking of developing a new lot and perhaps sharing a driveway. Good driveways make for good neighbors. Pick your neighbors and driveways wisely.

19

STANDARDS

We have many sacred rituals at our cabin. Events like the first campfire of spring at the lakeside fire pit. The first gathering on the deck after the snow melts away for good. The first fire in the wood stove on a frosty October evening. Most of them seem to be the endings or beginnings of some seasonal cycle.

One of the most sacred of these rituals is "putting in the dock." This wasn't always so. For many years I did not put the dock into the lake every spring. Because I just left my old-style wood section and metal post dock in the lake all year. It was used in the winter as a place of cold weather meditation, listening to the lake boom and crack, or as a seat to put on cross-country skis. If the ice twisted and heaved that old structure, I readjusted a few poles and moved on.

That simple practice changed when we "invested" a considerable chunk of funds in a roll-in aluminum dock. A friend in the dock business gave me a "friends and family" discount but it still was a major purchase. From that point on, I have partaken in the annual cycle of putting in the dock each spring and taking it out in the fall. I would note that ours might not be the first dock into the lake in our neighborhood, but I am the last diehard to roll it back out of the lake. I've even had to chip some ice a few times.

Part of this ritual is the gathering of the tools. There's a bit of elevation from the cabin down to the lake and younger legs are not always available to help. Prior planning prevents trips up and down the hill to the cabin and the frustrations that come with each unneeded trip.

First, I dig the old waders out from winter storage under the basement steps. Maybe they will hold up for one more dock job. Maybe the small leak in the left knee area has healed itself since last fall. Next is a bucket for the short list of tools needed. One big freakin' pipe wrench. One big freakin' adjustable wrench. One set of big freakin' sockets and the correct-sized ratchet handle, hopefully including the right sizes for dock bolts. One big freakin' hammer since you can't do much in the Northwoods without a big freakin' hammer to beat things into place. And finally, one beverage of the right size and type to celebrate the completion of the project. I prefer a big freakin' strong IPA from a local brewery. I might need something big and strong if the project goes bad.

Note that the dog helper to accompany you is optional and subject to your species of choice. I prefer a black Labrador retriever female which I always have hanging around.

With bucket of tools and refreshment in hand and the waders slung over a shoulder, I trek down to the dock site with the Labrador running ahead with her choice of "tools." Sage, the current retriever-in-residence, seems to prefer a bright orange rubber ball. I pull on the waders and pray for a leak-less wade while the dog flips the ball into the icy waters of Crooked Lake and amuses herself while I work.

There are people who do this work in gangs, moving down the shore from cabin to cabin and helping each other. Thus "dock day" becomes a noisy neighborhood celebration complete with music playing, libations before, during, and after the work, and maybe even a barbecue when all the docks are in. I prefer a quiet one-on-one experience with my dock, wrestling it into place and swearing in privacy with just the dog, who doesn't care about my choice of words. Even wife Marcie is not invited because she might have too many helpful suggestions while supervising from shore. This way the dock gets put in at my own pace, to my own standards.

The process and standards that dock installations are held to can vary greatly from dock owner to dock owner. I always judge mine by "Big George" standards. Big George was a shoe store tycoon from some southern state. I became acquainted with him during my college years in a locale not far from my cabin. His dock placement and the post-placement celebration were held to the highest standards.

A good friend of mine and I would be "invited" to assist in spring dock installation. The only promised compensation was attendance at the celebration that happened afterwards. This promise was always contingent on the work being "done right" and to his standards. Big George's dock was not the easy roll-in kind. I think this was a case of Big George having earned his money the hard way and an expensive dock was not needed if laborers like his son and us guys were available to supervise. And supervise he did.

The heavy treated-lumber dock sections were floated out into the spring waters without the benefit of leak-proof waders. As broke college kids, we could not afford both beer and waders. The dock sections were then propped up on steel posts and lifted to the correct height by sheer manual labor. I don't remember what the correct height-above-water was, but it was clearly stated and measured. The tools in Big George's dock placement list included a tape measure and a level that are lacking in mine. He used them, making sure each of the half-a-dozen sections were placed at the correct water height and were PERFECTLY level both lengthwise and widthwise. He was the classic perfectionist that I am not.

This may make Big George sound like a domineering pain-in-the-butt. But he wasn't. He had a style and means of communicating, whilst parading down the half-finished dock, holding a drink in one hand and a tape measure in the other. His commentary on our efforts was laced with politically incorrect humor and profanity that kept us laughing while we focused on the details. And when he had his back turned, we would get our jabs in, maybe even joke about loosening a bolt and watching him pitch into the cold lake with us. But we didn't. Like I said before, we worked for beer, drinks, and food. And Big George knew these things.

Big George knew how to be a host, how to entertain guests, and did it right even if they were lowly dock boys. The beer served was some sort of dark Bock beer in bright red cans from his southern hometown—beer unheard of in Minnesota at the time, at least to keg beer-swilling college kids. That's where I found out about real beer. A cocktail, if that was your preference, was a gin and tonic made by him, for you, with the good top-shelf stuff in the right amounts. That's where I learned about a real gin and tonic. All the while the grill was going. The thick loin-cut pork chops and steaks, served up after the dock was very correctly placed, are legends in my mind.

So that's the stuff I think about, by myself, while not so carefully placing my shiny aluminum dock over the course of only about a half-hour, or maybe forty-five minutes if it fights me a little.

Without a tape measure and level, it might be just a little cockeyed one way or another. Just "eyeball-level" good. I might have to adjust it later if it doesn't meet Marcie's standards or if the neighbors start mentioning the slight list to one side. But that can wait until warmer water without the need for leaking waders.

I then climb back onto the shore-side deck section and remove the waders. Yup, that leak in the left knee hasn't fixed itself yet. Now comes the final steps in dock placement according to "Mike's Standards."

I pop open my celebratory beer and offer a salute to Big George, wherever he may be now some fifty years later. Then I pick up the orange bouncy ball that Sage has dropped at my feet. She knows the final step of dock installation and it's up to her to get it done.

If it's a good year, and if my arm remembers the correct amount of effort, the ball bounces off the last board of the dock and goes airborne high over the water. Sage follows at a dead run and likewise goes airborne, pushing off from the last board, catching the ball at the top of the bounce and splashing down into the depths of Crooked Lake.

Dock's in!!!

FIREWOOD PROGRESS

I'm a big fan of the many Reality TV shows that depict life in rural Alaska and the far north of Canada. I realize that "Reality TV" doesn't always relate to real reality. I've got a close personal friend who works in producing shows of this genre. He tells me stories about how "real" some of them are. I would further note that while I like watching people working hard to enjoy this simple backwoods lifestyle, I refuse to watch the show that depicts some truly sad people living in the Alaskan bush and acting real stupid for the camera. I am selective in what I watch, keep an open mind, and enjoy the scenery and some of the things I have in common with these people.

One common theme seems to run through these shows: hardy people striving to make progress, to make their lives easier one project and one day at a time. A better cabin. A better dog sled. Or a bigger, better outhouse. An often-repeated refrain is—"We need to make progress so that we can make life easier and live this lifestyle into our senior years."

That's something I can relate to. I'm not getting any younger either.

These folks do seem to have an advantage over me even though I don't live as far north as they

33

do. Progress in their struggles seems to be aided by the television dollars I assume they get paid for allowing us voyeurs into their lives. Every season their equipment changes to newer, better, and more modern. The battered old boat seen on the show for years gets replaced by a new bigger boat, maybe even a sweet custom-built one. Snowmobiles (or snow machines as they erroneously call them) change from twenty-year-old smoke-belching wrecks sporting cracked windshields and rotted seats to racy-looking new sleds with heated handlebars and electric start.

Most of all, I can relate to their struggles with gathering firewood, especially the chainsaw problems. Their rusty old saw from "last season" has been replaced by a newer bigger one with a Scandinavian name, a chainsaw that I openly lust over. Despite this upgrade, most weekly episodes still depict these TV stars struggling with the saw— new or old. Or as the narrator dramatically states —"This firewood is crucial to their survival in the coming brutally cold Alaskan winter. If the chainsaw can't be fixed, there will be no firewood to warm their freezing bodies and they face a long, slow, cold, untimely death at their remote Alaskan cabin."

Now I think that most of them, except for maybe that really dumb tribe, would be smart enough to get out of Dodge if the chainsaw don't start and the firewood runs low. They could always hitch a ride with the camera crew that's following them around. I'm pretty sure the TV networks aren't gonna let the camera crew and expensive equipment die a long, slow, cold, untimely death in the Alaskan wilderness next to the frozen lifeless bodies of the stars of their hit show. But the labor and the struggles to put up an adequate supply of firewood look to be real, at least to a point.

My struggles with firewood and chainsaws have been well-chronicled in books and magazines, even if I haven't yet secured a lucrative TV show gig. And just like these guys and gals, I'm not getting any younger. Maybe I said that already. In any case, I'm always looking for ways to make the whole firewood experience easier.

Given my plans to spend a year, or two, or ten, working on a cabin addition, I recently decided to make some progress of my own. I had acquired a huge lot of unprocessed firewood, also known as "logs," from two sources. One was a county road clearing project. The County had left a big stack of trees neatly piled only a half a mile from the cabin. This pile included some prime oaks that had been in the way of progress. I asked for and received one of the few coveted firewood permits for the pile. I had to move fast. The other permit holders saw this pile as an easy remedy to their firewood problems and lusted over the same oak logs. We have also had a problem in the area with the theft of firewood. Not everyone believes in permits.

I got the jump on the competition and moved

a significant portion of six-foot logs to a new pile alongside the outhouse. Enough for three- or four-years' worth of firewood. But six-foot logs are not yet true firewood. They need to be sawed into sixteen-inch lengths, split, stacked, and dried before being stuffed into the cozy space of my little wood stove in the dead of a brutally cold Northwoods winter.

My neighbor and I had also recently labored to construct a new shared driveway through the woods to our cabins. Clearing that three-football-fields-long path in dense forest had generated my half of something like three-hundred-fifty former trees, now reduced to more six-foot logs. My frugal Scandinavian genes and firewood demands would not allow all that potential firewood to rot away in the forest. The driveway logs were now heaped together with all those other logs in that mountainous pile alongside the outhouse, needing to be sawed, split, and stacked so that they would assist in saving me from a long cold death in the freezing confines of a firewood-less Northwoods cabin. And I wasn't getting any younger. Maybe I already mentioned that . . .

I made an executive decision. It was time for a new method of log splitting. Something faster and less labor-intensive than my trusty old eight-pound manually operated splitting mall. It was time to make progress.

I noticed that my neighbor, my partner on the

new driveway, had the same firewood issue. He is younger than me, but that doesn't mean he is young. I also observed that a couple of my nephews had recently built a nice place just down the road. They seemed to have plenty of potential firewood laying around. However they were still young and they had busy lives which meant dealing with firewood was low priority. I made these guys a proposal. I'd research and buy a gas-powered hydraulic log splitter. They could chip in for the capital purchase cost and enjoy the firewood progress. They agreed.

I've proven over the years that I am not much of an expert on small gas-powered equipment. Unlike those Alaskan TV stars, my life doesn't depend on quirky gas-powered engines starting and operating at 60-below zero. I do know a real expert in this case. My friend Bill has spent a lifetime selling farm equipment, large and small, including log splitters. He needed to get out of the house and was willing to take a road trip to investigate a used log splitter, share his expertise, and buy me lunch. He still owed me for taking that old pontoon boat off his hands a couple years ago.

The used splitter we viewed was too used for my taste and seemed expensive given its questionable condition. Bill used it as an example to educate me on things like hydraulic cylinder size, controls, and especially the brand of motor. He clearly preferred the motor made by a foreign company that is well known for its dependable motorcycles, cars, and trucks. I'd get more explicit and name the company but then you'd think that I'd sold out like some of those reality TV stars.

"These motors start when you need them to start and they last forever," said Bill.

I tend to lean towards Scandinavian companies when it comes to chainsaws and the like, but I noted his advice. I do like engines that start and keep on running.

Now that I was an expert in log splitters, I started the search for one that would fit the budget the other guys had approved. First, I chased ads for used machines on the usual internet-based market sites. We all know how that works. Make a call, leave a voice mail, and never hear back from the seller. Or send a text and get a message back—"It sold a couple weeks ago—no longer available." Or most frustrating, the following scenario. Approve the deal over the phone or internet, drive fast to a bank ATM, withdraw cash, and race to the seller's house, only to find him standing in his driveway counting cash from a guy that showed up unannounced a few minutes before you and paid just a little bit more than you had negotiated.

I gave up on this method and made an early morning trip to the local farm-fleet-hardware-sporting goods store. I arrived just as the staff were unlocking the doors. A nice young guy who claimed to know something about log splitters took me outside to their selection and gave me a sales pitch.

"This one has the motor you like and is only fifty dollars more than the others. But it's our only one in stock with that motor and it will sell fast. Do you want it or not?"

It was within the budget I had established with the other guys. I fell for his high-pressure sales pitch. "Yes," I said. "I'll take it."

I know I shouldn't gloat but since this rarely happens to me, I must. As we were filling out the paperwork, another guy walked up, looked at us in disbelief and said—"I wanted that one. I saw it on your website and just drove fifty miles to get it!"

I struggled to keep my mouth shut but managed. The young salesman rolled his eyes and replied, "You should have called first. How was I supposed to know you were coming? Let me finish here and then maybe we can hunt down another one or order one."

I hitched my new purchase to the truck, pulled it back to the cabin, and got busy making firewood before my neighbor and nephews showed up and wanted to play with the new toy. Call me selfish but I don't want to experience a long, slow, cold, untimely death in the brutal Northwoods winter. I'm not getting any younger and I haven't got a TV crew to help me out.

THE TRUE COST OF FIREWOOD

My travels researching stories and selling books, sometimes at the same time, are often done on what many would call a "low budget." Book sales have been good to me but that doesn't mean I'm getting "Steven King-rich" or anything close to that. Luckily these trips are often to places where high quality food, drink, and lodging are available at low cost if you are the adventurous sort.

On a recent trip, I found myself at the very end of the Gunflint Trail. Literally the end of the road. I could probably see Canada, somewhere over there in the haze. Let's talk about high quality lodging accommodations. I was on a campsite four or five stories above the Seagull River as it roared downhill from Seagull Lake, tumbling over rapids and small falls, headed towards the border. Forget that my sleeping quarters were a one-man tent I bought at a clearance sale. It was a room with a million-dollar view and ambiance. The campsite fee was only eleven dollars for the night given the already low Forest Service fee was cut in half by the "Golden Age Passport," or as I call it the "Old Peoples' Card," in my possession. Thanks again to those who had the foresight to preserve places like this for all to enjoy.

The Last Cabin

It's true that I did have other expenses for food, drink, and other critical supplies. I had stopped in Grand Marais and got provisions for the trip up the long and winding road. A crowler of fine locally brewed beer—ten dollars including tip at the brewery. A filet of brown sugar-smoked lake trout and a couple strips of candied salmon from the local fish market—fifteen dollars. A loaf of rosemary bread fresh from the bakery—six dollars. And finally, the real indulgence, three bundles of locally sourced firewood from a convenience store—eighteen dollars.

If you count that I had enough food for leftovers for the next day and thereby avoided the cost of some unhealthy but irresistible fast-food lunch, the firewood was the most expensive part of my stay. I set up camp and hiked down to the river to get a close-up look before sunset. Then, exhausted from a hard day of selling books, I sat down at the campfire ring in a comfy chair and built a campfire to enjoy. Or I should say I attempted to build a campfire.

Keep in mind that I consider myself somewhat of an expert, a connoisseur, on the subject of firewood. Maybe the following words will seem a bit harsh to those who are less knowledgeable.

To get right to the point, this wood was nothing special. The supplier was delivering a fresh load as I made my choices among the stacked bundles. I would have preferred a mix of aspen, birch, and a hardwood like oak, ash, or maple. In this case I could have any wood I wanted, as long as it was birch. While some birch is great in the campfire or wood stove, it tends to be smoky even when dry and aged. This stuff was neither dry nor aged. It was heavy and damp to the touch. But I didn't have an option if there was going to be a campfire. So, I picked through the bundles, making sure that each of the three chosen ones had a few small sticks to get the fire going and some bigger stuff to sustain the blaze.

My initial assessment of this so-called firewood proved correct. Getting the fire going and keeping it blazing was a full-time job. I sipped my local brew while tending the weak, flickering, smoky flames and contemplated the true cost of firewood.

Each of the three bundles I purchased held about ten sticks of wood of varying diameter, averaging sixteen inches in length. I am guessing that a better mathematician would find that each bundle averaged around three-quarters of a cubic foot of wood. That happens to be an industry standard for campfire bundles. From there let's consider a comparison to good quality wood, the kind you, not me, might have delivered either for your wood stove or campfire ring. Forget about those small quantities called a face cord or fireplace cord and move on to the true measure—a full cord.

The Last Cabin

When properly stacked, this should measure eight feet long by four feet high and four feet wide. That measures up to about one-hundred-seventy bundles of the six-dollar-per-bundle stuff from the convenience store. If we use convenience store prices, that full cord would cost you $1,120 dollars. There might be some sales tax involved too.

I had to pull out my smart phone to do the calculations for that bit of information. Note that said phone was pretty much useless as a phone, given that these sites don't come with free Wi-Fi and cell phone coverage ended somewhere back down the Gunflint Trail. But the sun setting to the west, over the river, through some towering thunderheads was worth a picture on its camera as long as I had it out.

Let's compare "real firewood" prices to that cost-per-bundle total. In my neck of the woods, a full cord of good dry mixed hardwood is going to cost around three-hundred dollars delivered. I typically burn around three cords of wood per year in the cabin's wood stove and some extra in the campfire ring. So that thousand-dollars-plus cord of bundled wet birch would cost about four times more than the good stuff, even with delivery.

I try to pay as little for my firewood as possible just like my road trip accommodations. Thus, I never have firewood delivered. I forage on my own acreage, get permits from the local authorities to haul logging leftovers back to the cabin, and once in a great while I pick up bundles of slab wood from the local sawmills. That sounds cheap, even for the forest stuff, since a permit only costs thirty-five dollars, and is good for nine cords or around three years' worth of wood. Of course, there are other costs.

There's hauling expenses, using my truck and trailer and gas. Next comes the sawing, splitting, and stacking process. And finally, the question of what my labor is worth needs to fit into the "what's the real cost" equation.

What is my labor worth in this calculation? Many people would say I've got nothing better to do so it's free. After all, here I was, lazily burning boughten firewood while watching a couple of guys fishing on the bank of the river below me. They must have got firewood from the same place. They tended a smoking fire while watching bobbers and swatting at bugs. Maybe that was the best use for this lousy stuff—bug repellent. I would note that I didn't have bugs at my fire whether it be because of my lofty location above the river or the smoldering wood.

One of the main expenses in the processing equation is the chain saw. I recently upgraded from the cheap foreign-made saws I usually buy and swear at, to a genuine made-in-Sweden model. You might call that a foreign made one too but that doesn't consider that I'm at least half Scandinavian, part of which is Swedish. Therefore, I don't consider that foreign. It cost me one-hundred seventy-nine dollars and ninety-nine cents, plus tax. I know that years later because I left the price sticker attached to educate my sons and other users about the true cost of maintaining a cabin and making firewood. Let's figure that at around fifteen dollars per cord if we do a ten-year amortization and add a little bit for gas, oil, and chain sharpening.

Good thing I still had the smart phone available to help with that calculation. Especially since I got distracted by a beaver swimming in the pool below, slapping his tail at those two fishermen, clearly asking them to return to their campsite so he could get to work on his own tree-cutting project.

Now comes the real work—splitting the wood into usable-sized pieces. I used to pride myself on splitting each piece of firewood the old-fashioned way—slamming it apart with an old-fashioned manual splitting maul. But I'm not as young as I used to be. And neither is my next-door neighbor Tom, who also burns a fair amount of wood. So, I coerced him and a couple of my technology-loving nephews into buying a gas-powered log splitter. If we amortize my share of that over our ten-year-period, punching some more buttons on the smart phone tells me the splitter adds maybe ten dollars per cord. This low figure leads me to question why we didn't buy this splitter long before. Because that seems cheap when compared to shoulder replacement surgery and the splitter is fun and addictive to operate.

With my smart phone calculator handy and ready, I added a few more sticks of "firewood" to the smoldering fire and totaled things up. If we assume my time is worthless, my home-grown wood costs about twenty-five dollars a cord, give or take a dollar or two for my campfire/beer/food-influenced calculations. How's that for a bargain compared to three-hundred dollars per cord to have someone do all that work for me? Or the more than a thousand dollars per cord that I'd pay for this lousy wet birch that was smoking up my campsite? That's true Scandinavian frugality!

I was tempted to put all these calculations into words and send the firewood supplier a nastygram about the quality of their work and the cost of their product. But that didn't seem to be a very nice way of handling a complaint and I'm sure these are good hard-working North Country folk. Perhaps better would be to invite him or her to the campfire, share some food and drink, get to know each other, and have a polite conversation about firewood quality and philosophy.

"Think about this," I'd say, waxing philosophic with an after-dinner brew in my hand, "if you sold better wood that was dry, didn't smoke, and actually burned, people would stay up later at their fires and burn more wood, because it would actually burn, and maybe you would sell more firewood and make more money!"

But I know I shouldn't do that. I learned a long time ago that some people are better at arguments than others. He or she would probably reply with something like this: "Here's the way I see it. Perhaps the quality of my wood could be better. But in this case having the opportunity to buy firewood allowed you to spend a night drinking fine beer and eating fine food around a campfire, on the edge of a wilderness, with the river's muted roar below, the sunset to the west through some towering thunderhead clouds, while a beaver swims in the river and entertains you by slapping his tail. Have you really got anything to complain about?"

He or she would be right.

TROUBLE IN YELLOWSTONE

I have plenty of fun, adventure, and sometimes misadventures while hanging around the cabin and traveling the Northwoods. But sometimes Marcie and I hit the road and see what we can find in other parts of the world. Take for example Yellowstone National Park. I got into big trouble out there a few years ago.

No, I didn't feed the bears, step off the boardwalk at Old Faithful, try to pet a buffalo, or even take a selfie with a nasty old bull elk. All I did was call the mule deer doe that was snoozing in the sun in front of our rental cabin "tame." A female Park Ranger overheard the remark and gave me a public lecture on how the park's wild animals were indeed "wild" and not to be messed with. Or insulted, I guess.

I had to do some back-tracking to convince her that I was not just another dumb tourist. And by the way, take my advice and don't publicly call "bison" by their common name of "buffalo" either. That will cause more trouble. But they'll always be "buffalo" to me. Sometimes I just feel like a rebel.

In Ms. Park Ranger's defense, Marcie and I soon learned that not all of Yellowstone's wildlife conveniently hangs out near the back door or in the parking lot. I did have to slowly weave the truck around buffalo calmly sauntering down the road through the Lamar Valley, guided by the white stripe painted down the middle of the road. And elk sunbathed on sidewalks in Mammoth, oblivious to the tourists gawking and pointing cameras at them from just feet away. But to see wild things doing wild things, more effort was usually required.

It was also apparent that we were ill-equipped for the experience. The mess of gear packed into the truck included two pairs of run-of-the-mill tourist-quality binoculars. Our first evening was spent at a Yellowstone River overlook in the Hayden Valley, a miles-wide expanse just north of Yellowstone Lake. Several senior-age ladies were comfortably relaxing in canvas chairs, enjoying the views through high magnification, tripod-mounted telescopes, AKA "spotting scopes."

Our binoculars allowed us to watch eagles flying down the river and two playful buffalo calves parting the waters of the river as they charged across. We could see the big pictures. The ladies with the spotting scopes could see individual wing feathers flexing in the wind on the eagles' wings. They could see water droplets and mud flying from the hairy buffalo calves. All from the comfort of their chairs without straining their eyes. Luckily, they were willing to share these views with us and many other tourists from all over the world. We returned to this spot night after night to enjoy the camaraderie and soon developed a strong appreciation for the wild side of a park. A side that is often knocked for crowds and those "tame" animals mentioned earlier. Better prepared we would be, come the next time.

There was a next time. A couple years later Marcie was using her own high-quality zoom lens spotting scope with an angled eyepiece, her own tripod, and a newly purchased Wal-Mart canvas chair. Note to self—remember not to leave our chairs leaning against the wall of the garage back home next time. I had a cheap straight eyepiece spotting scope I got on sale, a borrowed tripod, and my own new cheap chair. We organized ourselves and got ready for action. A half-a-dozen or so less well-equipped visitors gathered around us and asked about the view.

Across the river, over half-a-mile away, a lone wolf pup was playing. He was just a shapeless black dot to the other guys and gals equipped with only their eyes or binoculars. But dial him in on our spotting scopes and he was a playful puppy practicing hunting skills by catching grasshoppers, bouncing up and down and over a small ridge. This was entertaining, but then came the big show.

One of the other onlookers pointed and yelled —"Hey—look at this!"

Two adult wolves, one an ebony black and the other a traditional gray, were loping down the valley with bushy tails streaming behind. They hooked up with the puppy and spent the next fifteen minutes playing like best doggie friends at a suburban dog park, rolling, wrestling, and wagging tails. When they left, the pup was in the lead, playfully quartering in front of the proud parents. It was a Yellowstone moment, captured in detail thanks to the power of my cheap spotting scope.

The fun didn't stop when the wolves left. Snow-white pelicans drifted down the lazy river and perched on driftwood. Rusty-feathered mergansers slept on islands with heads tucked beneath wings. Dinosaur-like sandhill cranes stalked tasty bugs in the olive-gray sagebrush. A mile away, on the far side of the valley, herds of elk wandered in and out of the tree line. Closer to the river, small groups of buffalo scattered about with young bulls playfully butting heads, cows nursing calves, and big bulls rolling in the dust.

When viewed with binoculars they were interesting birds and animals, but monotone and lacking in detail. In contrast, our new spotting scopes drew them closer, allowing our eyes to discover colorful individuals with blinking eyes and ruffled feathers or dust billowing and collecting on shaggy fur coats.

The spotting scopes had another advantage learned on our previous trip. Their magnification could draw in creatures from across the river valley and let us marvel in their individual behaviors and looks. They also drew in people. Park visitors from across the nation and from across oceans and continents were attracted to their novelty. They wanted to see what we were seeing.

It started with a retired sheriff from Nebraska and his spouse, equipped only with under-powered binoculars like we once were. Casual talk about mutual interests lead to sharing the spotting scopes with them for the next three nights. Many tall tales about hunting, fishing, and the pursuit of criminals were told when the wildlife action was slow.

Families came too. Nothing will make you a hero with vacation-stressed parents quicker than letting their children share the view through your spotting scope. The pelican or cow elk that you have grown tired of watching is a new discovery for kids bored with staring out a mini-van window. We swapped bad weather and vermin stories with a couple from Louisiana while we tutored their children on spotting scope use. They easily bested our Minnesota thunderstorm and mosquito tales with stories of hurricanes, alligators, and venomous snakes. Another family from Michigan with three youngsters joined us night after night and let Marcie and me practice our grandparent skills.

Next came a parade of nations, drawn to the spotting scopes to see the wonders of Yellowstone up close and personal. First was a family group from Switzerland. The mother, a second-time Yellowstone visitor, was leading her parents and two children equipped with only palm-sized binoculars. An athletic young couple from Belgium stopped by for an evening and left us seriously jealous of the adventure they were chasing, traveling across the West, visiting as many national parks as they could. We shared adventures and improved international relations with other folks from France, Russia, and Japan while sharing the views of those spotting scopes. Perhaps the United Nations and a few other world powers should meet at Yellowstone, at a Hayden Valley overlook, with the river passively flowing below, and share the view . . .

Unfortunately, some folks did abuse this power. A thirty-something lady, obviously what I started calling a "Ranger Rick Wannabe," perched on the rock railing of the overlook with her spotting scope for several nights. She kept up an endless and repetitive stream of chatter on the life and times of the wildlife in the valley behind her. Some of it was interesting—the first time. My degree in Biology and day job in the environmental protection field allowed me to mentally note that much of the rest was twisted half-truths and/or myths.

Then there was "The Guy," a truly classic Ranger Rick Wannabe. He had a high-tech spotting scope and camera worth thousands of dollars. He also had a wardrobe to match. Think hundreds of dollars' worth of African Safari clothes here. He was more reserved in his info sharing but had a twisted sense of travel time in Yellowstone and should have refrained from providing "expert" advice. I heard him tell the father of a mini-van full of family that the Lamar Valley, on the far edge of the park, was full of easy-to-find wolves and bears and was only "a half-hour drive" away. Having done that trip earlier in the day, I waylaid the father before he left and told him he was facing an hour and a half drive over Washington Pass on high, twisty, turny roads with less than an hour of daylight left.

Sharing equipment had other rewards beyond personal satisfaction and the camaraderie of fellow visitors. A web of grateful people spread out from the overlook and began returning with useful information. Stuff like where bears were hanging out. Where wolves were denned up and posing for photographs. Even a few tips on where the fish were biting. At one point I mentioned a desire to find a big bull elk. That family from Michigan mentioned earlier drove back from ten miles down the road with one of the kids exiting the van waving a camera. He ran over to show me a photo of a real beast of a bull elk and shared where to find the monster.

The best of all, or maybe the worst, or maybe just the most memorable, was yet to come. It was the Yellowstone moment that left me shaking my head and believing some of the stories about the stupid things some people do in Yellowstone. And this time it wasn't me.

The same young kid that brought me the elk picture wandered off the overlook and up the sagebrush- and buffalo-poop-pie-covered hill behind us. He came running back, yelling—"Mike, Mike, come and see quick! There's a grizzly bear!"

The result of this announcement was a stampede of the twenty or so wildlife watchers that had gathered around us. They didn't run for the safety of their cars and lock their doors. Twenty or so people, mostly adults, ran up the hill, through the prickly sagebrush, dodging buffalo pies, to meet the reported grizzly bear and shake hands. They left the retired sheriff and me (and our smarter than average wives) standing alone in the parking lot, not believing what we were witnessing. My young friend persisted as he headed back up the ridge with his dad, "Mike, come on! There really is a big grizzly bear!"

I will admit that I overcame my strong sense of common sense and succumbed to the peer pressure of a ten-year-old kid. "Well," I told the sheriff, "I'm going to cautiously check out what is hopefully just a buffalo butt sticking out from behind a tree."

By now the crowd was silhouetted on the crest of ridge, shading eyes from the sun, and pointing off into the distance. I hiked uphill and saw my first grizzly bear of the trip. Luckily it was not an up-close and personal encounter with a protective mama bear with several cubs or a cranky old boar guarding a fresh-killed elk dinner. There, maybe a couple of football fields away, was a solitary grizzly, padding along a tree line, stopping occasionally to flip over a rock or rip a stump apart with long powerful sharp claws. I watched for a few minutes, took a couple of typical tourist pictures (yes, that blob right there is really a big old mean grizzly bear) and headed back downhill to separate myself from the tourist herd.

Halfway down I met a young lady, a Park Ranger. An official one, not a Wannabe. She was struggling up the hill as fast as she could, arriving late to the big party. "Is there really a grizzly?" she asked, while stopping to gasp for breath.

She groaned and uttered a very bad word when I assured her there was. I quickly added that it wasn't close and was calmly heading the other way. She resumed her climb at a slower pace while muttering some more bad words. I'm sure she was more professional once she reached the crowd, "educated" them, and shooed them down the hill.

I'm reminded of that incident with every news report mentioning an animal/human interaction that didn't go well for the human. It further reinforced what those brave, hardworking, usually patient Park Rangers go through day after day during the tourist season. I'm willing to bet the Rangers, the real ones, have an unofficial slogan for the park which won't show up in any public literature. It probably goes something like this—"Yellowstone Park—the only place on earth where people run to MEET grizzly bears."

"ICE"

"ICE"

On a sunny July day, Marcie and I met the oldest son and daughter-in-law at a local brewery to try a few good brews, hang out on the patio, and snack on wood-fired pizza from the food truck. Along with the IPAs and the fire-roasted goodness, we got a heaping helping of nostalgia, with some mystery thrown in as a side dish.

While inside the brewery getting a refill, Marcie called me over to a wall covered in paintings and photos by local artists. "Look at this," she said and pointed.

The object of her attention was a bright old-timey-looking sign that advertised a long-gone general store and gas station on a local lake. "FREE PARKING" it headlined, despite the fact there probably wasn't a parking meter in the entire county now or seventy-five years ago. The store's name was prominently displayed along with an antiquated six-character phone number from some old rural party line. It then got down to business and offered "General Merchandise, Candies, Cigarettes, Beer, Soft Drinks, and 'ICE.'" All straightforward except for a pin-up style, scantily clad young lady holding a drink pictured above the words—"Close Cover For Safety."

The Last Cabin

The business name brought back a wave of memories. In the late '60s, my next-door neighbor Rick and I used to cruise the neighborhood on weekend afternoons, filling his '62 Chevy Impala with other kids for a ride to the lake and an afternoon of fun on the beach. Since we were teenaged boys, we tried to fill the car with as many teenaged girls as would fit. The store was just up the road from the beach and was our supplier of "Candies and Soft Drinks" since we were yet too young for the "Beer."

Marcie and I already had a significant collection of lake-related signs hanging on the cabin walls. But they would have to move over and make room for this trip down memory lane. The tap master had the phone number of the artist. I dialed her up and found she was more than happy to part with the piece for a reasonable price. She came on down to the brewery to complete the transaction. We bought her a beer and asked for more info on this work.

Her inspiration was an old matchbook cover, probably from around 1950, that showed up in a collection a friend gave her. She enlarged and reproduced it as a bright yellow and gold collage with paint and paper inserts. That answered some of the questions we had. The store must have handed out matchbooks for advertising.

But the young lady pictured on the cover and her state of undress was perplexing. The artist related that she wanted to keep the piece family friendly and had changed the original by adding a thin white negligee to the model. I had assumed the lady was wearing a swimsuit based on the lake theme and my memories of playing on the nearby beach with bikini-clad teenaged girls. But no, the artist showed me a picture of the original matchbook cover. The stylish young lady was wearing pretty much nothing at all, and she wasn't holding a drink. She was talking into an old-style telephone receiver while exclaiming in very small print "Why I'm Shocked!"

Now why was a family-owned general store handing out that kind of advertising in conservative rural Minnesota in the '50s? And what's the young lady shocked about? Was there some store-related local folklore that I was too young to have heard about back then?

The artist then added to the mystery. She pointed out the "ICE" highlight in quotation marks. "What's going on there?" she asked. "Why is 'ICE' the only word highlighted with the quotations? Some secret code?"

That too remained a mystery. When we brought the sign back home, I went looking for answers. I sent a picture of it to a friend and asked what he remembered about the place. He related spending many Sunday mornings at the store's drink counter with his dad. It seems this place was a Sunday morning gathering spot for a group of local guys. They'd drop the family off at church and then come to the store to play cards and unwind from a long week of work. Sometimes the kids were picked up from Sunday school and allowed free range of the store while the dads continued their card game.

But there was more going on than a friendly game of poker or whist. The store didn't have a liquor license and most bars weren't open on Sunday back then. However, if you were part of this known group of locals and asked for a cup of "ICE," it might, allegedly, come with some added powerful "flavoring."

That was a plausible answer to one of the mysteries of this unique piece and I'll try not to pass judgment on this establishment or its customers over it. But I'm still wondering about the store's questionable taste in advertising and that undressed young lady. What's she shocked about? Who's she talking to? Why is she still in her jammies? Is there more mystery, some local secret or legend to be unearthed?

I'd love to ask her once she gets dressed. But she's not talking from her spot on the cabin wall as I relive a few memories of long past summer afternoons on the beach. And ponder her mysteries while sipping a full glass of "ICE."

THE SECRET FALLS

I know places, most of them west of the Mississippi River, deep in the depths of mountainous national forests, where cabin-loving people like Marcie and me can rent historic cabins and live the mountain cabin life for a few days or a week. These places take some homework to find, and sometimes must be shared with fearsome creatures like coyotes, bears, and mice.

Our favorite rental cabin comes with extras like a natural stone veranda, a view of a trout stream, and a local bear just to make life more interesting. The mountains the cabin is nestled in also contain a secret. A thirty-foot-tall waterfall where giant brook trout live undisturbed in a mist-covered pool below. The falls are so secret that they are not flagged on Google Earth or any maps. I know that. I checked them. The stream barely shows on aerial photos, emerging from a high elevation swamp and winding down from the mountains to dry sage desert shimmering in the heat miles below. The trail to the falls, through the forest and mountains, isn't marked either. I know that too.

I know about this place because a friendly forest service ranger mentioned it to Marcie. Marcie was hanging out on the stone veranda, reading books, watching the resident hummingbirds fight over a nectar feeder, and keeping an eye out for the cabin bear. I had spent most of our three days in paradise indulging in the guilty pleasures of the trout stream across the dirt road. This was not one of your classic western trout rivers like the Madison, the Yellowstone, or the Bitterroot Rivers. It was a two-steps-across, willow-shaded tributary where a long cast with a fly rod gets nothing but branches and a snapped leader.

But if you sneak in low to the head of a mini-pool and surf a bead-headed nymph trout fly down the chute on a rod's length of line, there's a six, or seven, or eight-inch brook trout to be had on nearly every "cast." I thought I had invented a new form of fishing until I happened to read about that Japanese technique called "tenkara" and got educated. The Japanese have been fishing with this method for over four-hundred years. It's like fishing for sunfish with a cane pole and worms but with a fancier rod, a short length of line, and trout flies.

There's a bonus. As pretty as they are, brook trout are considered an invasive species in this part of the world since they fight for food and habitat with the native trout. Catch-and-eat is encouraged. Roll their red-spotted, white-finned carcasses in crushed Parmesan potato chips, toss into the cabin's well-seasoned cast iron fry pan with a little butter, and you have breakfast, lunch, and dinner.

But back to the falls where the forest ranger said giant brook trout live. She told Marcie that this was a place we needed to see. It was an easy hike —"it's only about fifteen minutes or so off the road and worth the effort."

When I returned from a morning of fishing, Marcie told me about the falls and we set off on what would become an epic adventure, a quest of biblical proportions.

We drove six or seven or eight miles on two-track mountain roads, parked at what looked like the right spot and headed out south across a wide expanse of high-country sagebrush, ready for the secret falls, and maybe even a refreshing clothing-optional shower in the falls. Why not? It was the middle of the week in the middle of nowhere with no one around.

The hike went on for over an hour. In the distance was a faint depression with greenery, the hint of an oasis in our sagebrush desert. But with only a couple of sixteen-ounce water bottles and the burning sun above, we admitted defeat and retreated. It's a pity that we hadn't heard about this wondrous waterfall earlier in the trip. We had to head out of the mountains the next morning and drive home without another chance to search. But I didn't forget about the cabin, the fishing—or the mysterious falls where there had to be big, fat, lazy trout. We had to return.

Sometimes these epic adventures take time. It

was over a year later when we returned to the cabin and tried again before I got too engrossed in fishing the cabin's trout stream. This time we tried a new approach route, driving south of the supposed falls and walking north to find them. We found the swampy headwaters of a small stream and a surprised herd of cow elk with their cute little calves. But no mystery falls. Just muddy warm potholes with a mix of elk tracks, cow tracks, and manure.

I had started to doubt whether the falls existed. Maybe they were just a myth to keep us gullible tourists coming back to rent campsites and cabins. I flagged down the forest service lady as she drove past the cabin and asked for more details and better directions.

"You know that dried water hole on the south side of the trail about eight miles from the fork in the road?" she asked. "Take the two-track trail just before it, drive to the fence line, and start walking. You really can't miss it."

Where had I heard that before?

We tried again, one more time. I took a left onto a four-wheel-drive trail right before a dried-up water hole and drove until a deep canyon and trees blocked the way. Then we hiked south through the trees and saw the Promised Land. Maybe.

We stood on the bare rock of the canyon rim, a couple hundred feet above the sound of running water. The source of the sound was screened by the pine trees and other assorted lush vegetation lining the canyon walls. The descent into the canyon looked challenging, scrambling down over rocky ledges, stepping through waist-high brush hiding God only knows what types of poisonous snakes, bears, wolves, and coyotes. It also looked like a great place for mountain lions.

"I ain't going down there," said Marcie.

I understood her doubts. But we were so close. "Give me half an hour. I'm not going back this time," I said.

Did I mention that I brought my fly rod this time? And a few bead-headed nymph trout flies? I braved the rocks and the brush, making plenty of noise along the way, hoping any snakes and other vermin would hear me coming and slink or sulk away from the commotion. There, after a sketchy ten-minute descent, I did truly find the Promised Land.

The steep walls of the canyon created a classic mini climate. While my wife roasted in the baking sun somewhere high above, I basked in the shade of vertical rock walls and evergreen trees coated in the mist of a mountain stream that was charging downhill, rolling over rocky rapids from pool to pool. And there were trout. Dumb ass brookies, staring up at me from the pools like sunfish off my dock back in Minnesota. I dangled a nymph in the face of one. It smacked it and came squirming out of the water on my lift.

Gone was the stealth needed back at the stream near the cabin. I hip-hopped from one slippery rock to the next, moving upstream from pool to pool, sun-fishing brook trout out on every ten-foot cast. Most were the same six-, seven-, or eight-inch beauties like the ones back at the cabin. Others weren't. Sometimes the rod would bend, and the fish would stay deep, bulldogging against the current, refusing to be horsed up out of the water. I landed twelve-inchers, thirteen-inchers, and lost some that had to be bigger. They were monsters. They got away, didn't they?

I couldn't resist smacking a foot-long specimen on the head, wrapping it in wet moss and stuffing it into a pocket for the trip back out of the canyon. It would be proof that I had found gold. Maybe it would entice Marcie to stay longer and brave the descent.

She was gone by the time I retraced my steps and climbed out of the canyon, well over my half-hour of allotted time. Lucky for me she had done some exploring on her own, searching for rocks and rattlesnakes on the canyon rim. I beat her back to the truck. However, she wasn't convinced that the adventure of the canyon was worth the fishing, and you may have noticed that I didn't mention finding the lost mysterious waterfall. Because I didn't. I got too wrapped up in the fishing and ran out of exploring time. Maybe the next day I'd leave the fishing rod behind and not get so distracted.

Maybe . . .

The trouble with waiting for tomorrow on adventures is that you never know what tomorrow will bring. In this case it brought two days of rain, wind, and thunderstorms. The ten miles or so of backcountry bad roads turned into impassable mud and washouts. We lounged around the cabin for our allotted time, enjoying the bird- and bear-watching, but never got a chance to continue our quest. At least for this year.

It was a couple more years before we were able to continue our quest. Sometimes these things take time, especially when you have jobs, family, and a cabin of your own to attend to. But the lure of the mysterious waterfall, hidden deep in the mountains and rarely seen by human eyes, was strong. We headed west once again. Just Marcie and me. This was starting to get personal. No one likes to admit defeat when it comes to epic quests for huge trout living below mysterious mountain waterfalls.

However . . . the role of Mother Nature in these treasure quests, or at least this one, cannot be understated. We had gotten to know the forest ranger lady in this location by now. We got to know both her and her husband on a first name basis. She gave us a warning as we stopped in the closest town to pick up the cabin keys.

"We had a nasty storm yesterday," she informed us. "The road into the mountains might be washed out or have trees down on it. You guys are going to be our scouts. Warn us about the road conditions if you can find phone service."

She also showed us a picture of the falls, proof that they existed and were as beautiful as advertised. We headed off on another adventure primed with new information and hope. Luckily, we were also driving my new off-road-capable SUV with the big tires, high clearance, and the rock-proof skid plates protecting the undercarriage. Because we needed all that. The forty miles of mountain roads into the cabin were filled with washed out gullies, new sharp-pointed road rocks and the occasional storm-broken tree branch. The SUV was up to the challenge and completed the trek, although there were some white-knuckle moments as I drove over and around obstacles while Marcie clutched the grab bar and expressed thoughts about the wisdom of her partner in adventure.

The next morning continued this theme and the weather pattern. We set off early, after a late-night thunderstorm provided us with a lightning show above the mountains and several more inches of rain. The road into the mountains consisted of ten miles of rocky washed-out four-wheel-drive trails that tested our marriage at several points. Especially the point where a road mud puddle in previous years was now a rushing mountain stream. The SUV forded the stream at full power, its exhaust rumbling, drowning out the exclamations from the passenger side.

The mighty SUV delivered us to our familiar trailhead intact. I once again pushed off on a solo quest. The ride to the trailhead was all the adventure Marcie needed for the day. She chose to stay behind with the truck and tip over rocks, looking for fossils and rattlesnakes.

The trip down into the canyon was getting to be familiar by now. I just had to roll the dice and make a decision once I got to the stream. Left or right? Upstream or downstream? Having gone downstream on the last trip, I chose upstream this time. But Mother Nature was making this trip more interesting down there in the canyon too.

The rocky mountain stream that I could usually hip-hop across on a couple of rocks was now a raging torrent from the thunderstorms. There was no getting across without the potential of being swept away, banging off rocks, and maybe even dropping off into oblivion should that mysterious waterfall be downstream. I didn't make it far before my stream-side path was blocked by deep swift water flooding up against a steep canyon wall.

I made the best of a bad situation. I fished back downstream until that route was blocked, catching a nice mess of brook trout in the flooded areas which normally were dry free-range cow pasture and elk habitat. It was then time to struggle back up out of the canyon, reunite with Marcie, and slide back down the trail to the cabin before more afternoon thunderstorms rolled in.

Those thunderstorms did roll in and kept rolling in overnight and into the next day. Sometimes I think I'm smarter than I look. Because I didn't try driving back to search for the falls in the next days, even with that tough SUV. It's not smart to travel alone in the mountains in bad weather and I sure wasn't going to get Marcie to accompany me again. Not this year anyway. We amused ourselves around the cabin, watching the hummingbirds squabble over the feeder, and watching out for the local bear, who seemed to like this cabin as much as we did.

Our next trip to continue this quest took a few more years before it happened. I'd say that this was getting personal now or that sometimes these things take time, but I think I've already used those lines. In any case, we hit the road again, this quest now having taken on a life of its own over the last ten years. You know the drill by now, we stopped in town to get the cabin keys, got more info from our forest ranger friend, talked hunting, fishing, and cabins with her husband, and trekked off into the mountains to our favorite western cabin retreat. The road was better this time.

The mountain road to the trailhead was also better the next morning. Marcie had no qualms about riding along, although I think she did so partially because we were driving HER new SUV and she wanted to protect it from drivers like me, ones that take too many chances (her opinion). This more modest SUV was up to the challenge and delivered us to the aspen-shaded trailhead without incident. Our only stop was to pet the friendly free-range ranch horses who stuck their heads in the window and requested that ears be scratched and an apple handed over as a toll to let us pass.

I dropped down into the canyon and headed downstream, convinced this was the way to that promised land. The stream was below normal level this year due to drought conditions. However, the fishing was as good as normal. I thoroughly enjoyed my hike, crossing the stream as needed and catching brookies in the pools. It got a little hot at one point. That was quickly taken care of by a dip in a pool alongside the trout. Life was good. But there was no hint of a waterfall, and I was eventually blocked by steep canyon walls and had to climb back out of the canyon, laden with trout for supper but no pictures of a waterfall.

I convinced Marcie to ride along again the next morning. I had to be close to the falls simply by the process of elimination. She also still had concerns about the use of her shiny new SUV. She packed her rock-hounding tools and a good book and we made our way back up the familiar mountain road to the usual spot.

This time I got more creative. I headed out across the rocky flats above the canyon, heading way to the left into new country. The trek took me through dry rock formations and flat outcroppings that resembled Mars or the moon, not anything you would expect to find a waterfall in. But once I cleared these obstacles, I had a view of the canyon from a distance and saw hope.

Our forest ranger friend had said—"Look for a spot that seems like a gash in the earth. A steep dark area that stands out from the hills and range land." There in the distance, I saw an area that reminded me of that advice. Of, course it was a mile away and in between were a few hills and valleys.

I found a valley that lined up with that dark spot and followed an elk trail as it sloped down towards the canyon. The sound of rushing water greeted me as I neared the canyon and its familiar trout stream. The sound was different this time, not the same as the stream in drought conditions experienced yesterday. I climbed uphill to a rock outcropping and finally saw the Promised Land.

Below me, the pine tree-shaded stream emptied from a notch in a vertical rock wall painted in natural multi-colors of orange, green, and yellow moss and lichens. The falls dropped some thirty feet straight down into a round boulder-lined pool, hidden amongst more vertical rock walls that formed a natural bowl-shaped amphitheater featuring the beauty of the falls. From there the stream emptied out through a narrow passage in the canyon, downstream to the area I had been exploring for years. It was as pristine and serene as imagined in many dreams.

I might have stayed there, just appreciating the view, or even found a way down to the pool for a quick refreshing dip in my undies or less. But as they say, all good things must come to an end. Or as you may have noticed by now, sometimes Mother Nature calls the shots, changes my plans, shows me who is in control. I felt a blast of wind hit from behind, followed by a rumble of thunder. Yes, there to the north was my nemesis from other trips. A nasty-looking storm was brewing and headed up the canyon. I had one last look at the new-found paradise, snapped a few pictures on the cell phone, and started hiking back. I hiked really fast!

Our personal forest ranger had often claimed that the hike to the falls could be done in fifteen minutes "or so." In this case I timed my retreat to the SUV at twenty-six minutes. Not a record by any means but not bad for an older guy being chased by lightning bolts and angry storm clouds. I made it to sanctuary right before the rain started and joined Marcie inside the SUV. We rode out the storm while I filled her in and reviewed pictures on the cell phone. She also had info.

While I was finding my way to the falls, two young lady ranchers showed up on their own adventure, seeking out the mysterious falls they had heard rumors about. Somehow, I had missed them on my "dash" back to the truck. They texted Marcie after the rain passed and thanked her for the information she had shared. They too had found what they were searching for and sent pictures of themselves playing in the falls to prove it.

I had to note the irony. After years of searching for the falls and never seeing another human being, I had been prepared to take a swim in the falls should they be found. Today I might have been cooling off in the clear waters, in undies or less, just as two young ladies discovered the natural wonder of the falls, and more. I'm glad I wasn't. That would have spoiled their view of paradise. Maybe Mother Nature had that in mind when she sent me running with the thunderstorm.

If so, Mother Nature was kinder the next day. The weather was better and there still was time for another adventure. I led the way back to the falls, urging Marcie on and telling her minor lies like "it's just past that next bunch of rocks," until we finally stood together on the rocks overlooking the paradise we had sought all those years.

Marcie chose to stay above and enjoy the

view. I picked my way down the rocky slope and up the creek to the fall's plunge pool. It had a spiritual feel that is hard to describe but comes with wild places like this. The roar of the falls, recharged from yesterday's thunderstorm, drowned out all other sounds, leaving me in my own isolated little world. On one side was a rock overhang with its walls blackened by many campfires. It wasn't hard to picture native peoples coming here on quests of their own, to meditate and consider life many centuries before me.

I didn't swim like I had planned. Partially not to ruin Marcie's view and partially in reverence to that sacred feeling of this place. I had brought the fly rod this time and set out to prove that giant brook trout did live in this idyllic spot.

I didn't catch a giant trout. However, I do have pictures to prove that trout live beneath the falls and can be caught by a low-tech fisherman like me, flipping out a ten-foot line with a simple fly at the end, practicing that centuries-old technique called tenkara.

If you happen to research tenkara further, you'll find that when it is translated to English from Japanese, it means something like "fishing from heaven." That seems fitting for places like this. Because here I was, "fishing from heaven" while fishing in heaven.

ISLAND OF NAMES

I was still a ten-minute hike from the harbor when I heard the Ranger Station's loudspeaker publicly send a radio message out to a long-departed National Park Service tour boat. The booming voice echoed the message off the steep sides of Isle Royale's Washington Harbor for all to hear.

"Windigo Harbor to Boat. We found Lisa. Let her friends on board know she's all right and will be spending the night here. We'll put her on a float plane to Grand Marais tomorrow afternoon."

Tell me more . . . You have my interest.

I made my way down the rutted hiking trail to the harbor overlook and plopped down on a bench to enjoy the view. Off in the distance, in a sheltered cove of the green coastline of Isle Royale, I could see my home-away-from-home, or cabin-away-from-cabin, if you will. The sailboat looked safe and secure, riding at anchor some fifty yards from shore. No need to hop in my orange kayak and paddle back just yet.

A lady ten years younger than me walked up and asked to share the bench. I know that personal info because we struck up a conversation and she offered that she was on a "landmark birthday" trip.

The Last Cabin

This day tour out to Isle Royale National Park was part of a larger Lake Superior birthday adventure trip. I asked her how it was going so far.

She was relaxed, happy, and willing to share her story. "It was going fine until I got lost on a hike out to the Grace Creek Overlook. I went the wrong way at a fork in the trail and ended up miles from here. Some young hikers got me squared away and tried to get me back in time. But I was too slow and missed the boat. I'm headed out on a float plane tomorrow to catch up with my friends."

I couldn't resist. "You must be 'Lost Lisa.' I heard about you over the radio loudspeaker."

She didn't even blush. "Yup, that's me!" She laughed. "I guess everyone knows me after that announcement. I've got a name and reputation now!"

The National Park settlement at Windigo is at the end of Washington Harbor, a long fjord-like channel poking into the interior of Isle Royale. It includes docks for Park Service tour boats and private motorboats and sailboats. There's also an Interpretive Center, campground, general store, and a few cabins for both tourists and employees. It has a frontier-like atmosphere with cell phone coverage nearly non-existent unless you hike miles to the heights of the island. Visiting means braving the big lake in your own boat, hitching a ride on a Park Service tour boat, or paying the price for a float plane ride from the mainland.

🐕

Island of Names

As Lost Lisa found out, it's still a place where an adventurous guy or gal can make a name for themselves based on their epic adventure or the epic misfortune that occurs as part of an epic adventure.

My own epic adventure started with a boat trip to the island, a two-day voyage from Wisconsin's Apostle Islands. My younger brother Steve takes care of a sailboat, a thirty-three-foot yawl with the name *The Yawl of America* painted on its stern. Minnesotans will probably get the joke . . .

I had a serious job on this adventure. I'd take care of the boat for seven or eight days while Steve and other volunteers of the Rock of Ages Lighthouse Preservation Society worked to restore the historic lighthouse guarding the southwest tip of Isle Royale. The lighthouse is a fascinating piece of Isle Royale history. See more about that at rockofageslps.org.

Our two-day trip across Lake Superior to Grand Marais and then on to Isle Royale was uneventful. The big lake was "flat calm" as us sailors say. We had to resort to the boat's little diesel motor instead of sailing, cruising the fifty or so miles across the big lake and then coasting down Washington Harbor to the Park Service dock. *The Yawl of America* is a classic 1970s custom-made boat with lots of beautiful woodwork. Much classier and distinctive than the other modern plastic and aluminum boats lining the harbor docks. Both the boat and Steve were recognized by many of the park staff, fishermen, and other volunteers hanging around.

Many of them greeted Steve, recognizing him as "Jim's brother." Our youngest brother Jim did the same adventure trip two years before with Steve and the boat. Forget that Steve had been trekking to the harbor for years as part of his volunteer duties. Jim and his outgoing computer salesman/writer/musician ways had left an impact on the regulars. He'd made a name of sorts for himself in his week-long stay, even if it was just plain old "Jim."

Steve didn't seem to mind. He's a rocket scientist after all and you can't let little things faze you when you're helping send people safely off into space or flying the latest jet fighter. I, on the other hand, took it as a challenge. I'd be spending the next week here, mixing with the locals and the tourists. Surely a semi-famous writer and outdoorsman like me could earn a name of his own, impressing the park rangers, tourists, and fishermen with my outdoorsy skills, humor, and wisdom.

I started making friends right away. A half-a-dozen ladies came down to the dock to enjoy the sunset. We were soon swapping adventures stories with them, although I will admit that our stories paled in comparison to their trips to places like Machu Picchu, European mountain ranges, and other exotic wild places.

I started calling them "The Wolf Pack." Isle

Royale is famous for wolves and moose and these ladies fit right in. They had just completed a week-long hike down the length of the island, backpacking and camping on their own self-guided tour. They were going to finish the trip canoeing and kayaking amongst the moose and wolves, and then hop on a float plane to Michigan to run a marathon. Try to keep up with that.

I asked Sarah, one of the Wolf Pack leaders, my patented, adventure conversation-starter question. "What was the most impressive thing you saw on the hike?"

She didn't have to think long—"When I almost walked into the ass of a moose."

Now that got my attention. I asked for more details.

"We were grinding along on the trail, hot, sweaty, and bug-bitten. I had my head down and was just trudging along in the lead, thinking about reaching our next campsite. Suddenly my friends started yelling. "Look up! Look out!" I looked up and found myself staring into a cow moose's butt from about five feet away. I could have walked right into it."

Luckily the moose was in a good mood and gave way to "The Wolf Pack." Maybe she didn't want to mess with this bunch.

The next day Steve anchored the boat in a secluded cove and disappeared, off to the mysterious lighthouse we'd passed on arrival to the island. I was alone to enjoy the surrounding area via the cheap little orange kayak I'd strapped to the boat's deck back in Wisconsin. How cheap and little? That bright orange piece of plastic cost me less than $150 at a Big Box home improvement center. Cheap, seaworthy, or not, I'd paddle it into the harbor early each morning, dragging a fishing lure behind. There I'd set off for some early morning hiking or maybe just hang around the docks and Ranger Station, mingling with interesting people, fellow islanders whether there for a day or a week or the season.

I'd be out-of-touch with friends, family, and most of the outside world for most of the time. Given the lack of cell phone coverage, the main source of worldly and local info is the marine radio in the Ranger Station. It's connected to a powerful loudspeaker that broadcasts weather reports, boat arrival announcements, and "Lost Lisa"-type communications out over the harbor and close-in waters.

Two different park tour boats cross the waters to the island to dock at Windigo on regular schedules, dropping off visitors and supplies. Some park at the dock for most of the day, allowing folks I soon called "day-trippers" to wander the grounds, visit the Interpretive Center, or to head off on short hiking adventures. These short adventures could turn into longer adventures if they missed the boat like

"Lost Lisa." The day-trippers were easy to distinguish from the hardcore backpackers. Day-trippers usually wore shorts and T-shirts and carried nothing more than a water bottle and a cell phone camera. The hardcore backpackers traveled in groups and were instantly sweating, sometimes struggling, as they made the hike up out of the harbor with their heavy packs of food and gear.

This relaxed schedule allowed me to get to know many of the long-term campers and park staff on a first-name basis. Among these was one of the tour boat captains, who had time to talk while waiting for supplies to be off-loaded or day-trippers to return. He was a crusty old salt, the type you'd hire to chase down a great white whale far out into the ocean. Or a great white shark should one show up in the clear fresh water of Lake Superior. Let's call him "Captain Quint" after that last guy. I really don't think he'll mind.

Captain Quint gave me a tour of his boat and named off a long list of sights I should see on Isle Royale. He also related a few adventures of sailing the sometimes stormy and treacherous waters of Lake Superior. Even when he wasn't docked at Windigo, I came to recognize his distinctive voice blaring out over the harbor's loudspeaker as he reported the boat's movements and noteworthy sightings.

My fellow park visitors were also an

interesting bunch and not just the adult types like Lost Lisa and the Wolf Pack. Windigo's meager amenities include a small general store. There you can pick from a small selection of basic fishing gear, food staples, craft beer, and "Pringles" brand potato chips. These canned stacked processed morsels of salty goodness are apparently what every hiker or camper craves on the island. The small confines of the store devote nearly an entire wall to rows and rows of every conceivable flavor. The store is also the only place in Windigo where you can get a hot pizza.

Basic but yummy pizzas are served on a first-come-until-they-are-gone basis during limited afternoon hours. Get there before it's gone, and you have a taste of home. Brother Jim had largely subsisted on these during his stay. I had to check them out and got there early.

Feasting on pizza at a nearby outdoor table were four boy scouts and two of their adult leaders. Feasting is probably a weak word here. These teenaged boys had just come off the trail after that week-long hike from one end of the island to another. Each was devouring his own family-sized pizza like a pack of Isle Royale wolves would consume a winter-killed moose in the cold days of March. Them pizzas didn't stand a chance . . .

They were bug-bitten and sweat-stained but still fired up about the adventure they'd had. I asked them my tried-and-true question. "What was the most memorable part of the trip?"

They mentioned wildlife, the bugs, and swimming in leech-infested water in the island's interior lakes. But then one of them pointed to a comrade and said, "Ask Outhouse Boy about his adventure."

Outhouse Boy readily related his adventure while stuffing down more pizza. The food or the water on the trip didn't agree with his digestive system. Maybe it missed a good pizza. He had spent much of his time in the primitive outhouses found along the interior trail. He hadn't wasted his time just sitting there.

"I developed an outhouse ranking system," he said. "From bad to worse, I've seen them all and can tell you where 'to go.'"

He further related his ranking system while his comrades and the adults shook their heads and laughed along. "While I was sitting there, I'd look around and count the holes in the walls, the number of spiders, mouse nests, things like that. Add that to the smell factor and I have them all ranked from bad to worse. I think the most spiders I counted in one was like seven."

Now that's one way to make the best of a bad situation and become a legend among your peers while you are at it.

The Last Cabin

I didn't spend all my time at the harbor or hiking in the forests above it. I put that orange plastic kayak to good use. The protected confines of Washington Harbor contain many secluded coves and small islands to explore. These come complete with sheltered sand beaches marked with wolf and moose tracks. Fishing isn't bad if you know basic things about trout, trout lures, and trout fishing, knowledge I've spent a life-time amassing. There are even a few shipwrecks if you get more adventurous and paddle down the five-mile-long channel close to the open water of Lake Superior.

About halfway down the channel is an interesting feature called "Jesus Rock." It's a rocky reef well off the island shore, almost a third of the way out into the otherwise deep channel. Most of the rocks lurk just half a foot under water. One small section protrudes just above the waterline, or just below it, depending on the current level of the big lake and the current wave height. It's called "Jesus Rock" for two reasons.

One, if the water level is just right, you could hop out of your boat or kayak and pretend to walk across water just like the Apostles claimed Jesus did back in the day. More dramatic would be if you were piloting a boat down the channel and suddenly ran aground on or narrowly missed the jagged rocks. You might then call out loudly, taking the name of some holy person in vain. I'm sure much more profane things have also been exclaimed out over the pristine waters of Lake Superior as Jesus Rock made itself known.

The day before my brother was set to return from his exile on "The Rock," as the lighthouse is known, I took an early morning paddle, fishing and exploring down the channel. Jesus Rock is a good place to fish. The morning was as foggy as Lake Superior can be, especially in the confines of the sheltered fjord-like channel. Visibility was maybe a few paddle strokes, fifty or a hundred feet. I cautiously coasted down the shore, just a paddle-length away from mist-covered cedar trees, and then glided the little orange kayak out to Jesus Rock. The fog was just starting to lift as the morning tour boat cruised down the channel, guided by Captain Quint and its radar and GPS.

I lifted my paddle in salute to the friendly waves of the tourists and kept on fishing. I didn't feel unsafe at all. I was right up on top of Jesus Rock's shallow reef. Its nasty jagged boat-ripping rocks were between me and other traffic. Any boat coming near me would find itself grounded and sinking long before it endangered my kayak. However, not everyone shared this opinion.

The next day the lighthouse volunteer boat roared up to *The Yawl of America* while I was enjoying my morning coffee. Brother Steve came aboard with his gear. He immediately informed me

103

that I was now as famous on Isle Royale as my friend "Lost Lisa."

He and the crew had been working on a restoration project and had their marine radio on, listening to weather forecasts and fishing reports. Something like the following was broadcast over the air waves and loudspeakers of Isle Royale, courtesy of my friend Captain Quint. "All boat traffic in the vicinity of Jesus Rock be on alert! There's some idiot in an orange kayak fishing out here in the fog!"

So, my week and a half on the island was not in vain. I caught fish, hiked, made friends, shared adventure stories with other adventurers, and became a legend that has not been forgotten. My brother has returned to Isle Royale since. Forget about "Lost Lisa," "The Wolf Pack," or "Outhouse Boy." They are history. But they are still talking about "The Idiot in the Orange Kayak."

"OFF MY GRID"
by Jim Lein

Author's Note—My brother Jim knows a thing or two about cabins, having lived in mountainous Colorado for most of his adult life and having visited many on his ski trips. He recently built a small one in the backyard of his home as a short getaway from all the happenings in the house. It's his little cabin-away-from-home right at his home. But sometimes that isn't enough. He longs for more. Here's his take on that.

"Off My Grid"

If I had my druthers, I'd shed the trappings of society and move into an off-the-grid cabin. "Off the grid" means different things to different people. For some it conjures up an image of a doomsday survivalist obsessed with stocking an impenetrable bunker with everything needed for his family to survive in isolation until the storm passes. That's not me and my family. We're at each other's throats three days into a week at a luxury resort. And that's with cable TV, maid service, and a swimming pool.

To others, "off the grid" means a pastoral life in a quaint farmhouse near Boulder with chickens, goats, an organic garden, and a windmill. Half a lifetime ago, that might have been me. But that ship sailed long ago. I can't get my kids to clean their rooms once a year. Imagine me telling them to weed the garden and scoop poop out of the chicken coop instead of watching *SpongeBob SquarePants* reruns after school. And my wife Jane, the lawyer and real estate agent? Picture her in a peasant dress milking a goat.

At my life stage, living off the grid would simply mean self-sufficiency. No mortgage, utilities, cable TV, Internet, or car payments. With five smartphone voice and data plans, our monthly phone bill is bigger than the mortgage on our first home. We're such high rollers at Costco that they offer us a free penthouse suite whenever we come to town.

Just give me the simple life. I flirted briefly with living off the grid when I was a ski bum. There was that week when my roommate Ziggy didn't pay the power bill. But we didn't suffer much because he charmed the two cute girls next door into letting us run an extension cord from their apartment to ours. And I lived in a Pontiac Firebird in the parking lot of the Frisco A&W for three months, but I guess you could say I cheated by using the bathrooms at the library.

I've never wanted a big house with all the latest electronic gadgets and more bathrooms than inhabitants. Jane, the real estate tycoon, has branded me a heretic and told her co-workers about my obsession with off-the-grid living. I've started looking over my shoulder. Someday I may be accosted at Safeway by an angry mob of associate brokers. If that happens, I'll just announce that I'm thinking about upgrading to a larger home close to dining and shops with a Mt. Evans view. That will throw them off the scent. I'll slip away while they're fighting over who found me first.

No, I'll never convert Jane to an off-the-grid happy camper. But we'll soon be empty nesters. Maybe my off-the-grid dream is within reach as a weekend refuge. It would have to be cheap. Cheap equals remote and almost inaccessible. Maybe a mining claim up above Empire. Just the ticket.

I love to daydream about designing and building my cabin. I am addicted to cabinporn.com. Yes, that's a real website featuring glossy, centerfold quality photos of cabins around the world.

My cabin will be designed to blend in with the environment so well that I'll have trouble finding it myself. To keep out the riff-raff and the lookie-loos, I'll set up a series of trials along the path—like a non-lethal version of what Indiana Jones encountered in the opening scene of *Raiders of the Lost Ark*. The first barrier will be a solar-powered, heated video gaming station with a mini-fridge under the chair stocked with Red Bull and Doritos. That will keep out all the Millennials. Next, there'll be a sign with very specific directions based on compass points and distance, like "walk north four-tenths of a mile and then turn east." This will confound the entire female gender since they only understand directions based on pointing fingers and proximity to landmarks. Like "turn that way at the Starbucks and turn this way when you get to Nordstrom's."

Finally, I'll pin a stack of two-for-one Hooters Happy Hour coupons to a tree. That'll send all the camo-garbed, AR15-toting rednecks scrambling back to their pickups. The seekers that pass all tests will find themselves at the entrance, a massive slab of thick pine panels bound with iron and sealed by a padlock like a medieval knight would put on a chastity belt. The key will be hidden under a welcome mat that reads "Wipe Your Paws."

The cabin will be constructed as much as possible from materials sourced from the property. In fact, my man cave could end up being a cave. If I'm lucky, there will be an abandoned Home Depot just down the trail. My boys would help me build it. I could pass on to them all that my father taught me. How to frame. How to insulate. How to nail down a wood floor. Wait a second . . . that was my neighbor Chip, not Dad.

Ahhh . . . what a life that would be. In the mornings, I'd linger in my bunk, envisioning what the day would bring. Skiing, hiking, or clearing brush off the ranch like Ronald Reagan would do. I'd steel myself to the cold, force my creaking bones to roll out and dash over to the wood stove to stoke it against the morning chill. In the evening I'd sit out on the porch and bask in the alpenglow as the sun sets over the Divide. Maybe one glorious twilight, my son would touch the shoulder of his old man and say in a soft voice, "Dad—it's getting cold. Time to go inside." But my spirit will have flown, leaving nothing but a smile on my face.

I can dream, can't I?

THE BOSS

The Boss

Working on the addition to the cabin has provided opportunities to post many photos to social media, keeping all my "friends" informed. The pictures show the cabin addition slowly, step-by-step rising from the ground as the background scenery turns from summer green to autumn gold to stark dead winter white. Lots of white, given the late summer start date and the arrival of one of the snowiest winters on record. Go figure. I try to build a freakin' cabin addition and gol dang it, it snows freakin' record amounts. Who would have ever thought that kinda crap would happen to me, darn it anyway?

Now if that sounds like pretty mild language from a guy who's royally teed off about bad weather, it's because I've been trying to back off on the attitude and swearing. My wife thinks it's gotten out of hand and even went so far as to comment on one of my posts that people should realize that "Mike is a crabby carpenter." Then she added, "And he swears a lot too." I was tempted to remind her that both our sons had told her that she's the one that taught them their first few cuss words. I wasn't sure what the reaction would be, so I didn't.

If I am crabby and profane, I have plenty of

reasons. Doing this much of the work, at this advanced age, in this nasty winter weather wasn't in my plans. Add to that certain curious people, who think they are trying to be helpful, asking too many dang stupid butt questions. Questions I can't answer because I'm busy working and haven't had time to think that freakin' far ahead.

Lest you think I grew up in a crabby, swearing family, let me assure you that I can't remember a nasty four-letter word ever coming from my dad's mouth. At least not a real swear word like $%^!!! or ^&*%!!! He did use "dang" and "darn" and other classic old-school Scandinavian farmer swear words and was famous among us kids for spelling out "H-E-double-toothpicks." But nothing like #$#% or ^&*@ and he certainly never took the Lord's name in vain and never, NEVER cussed at my mom. I'm pretty sure I've never even heard anything stronger than "darn" come from her. They didn't tolerate bad language from us kids either although I'm sure a few of us tasted soap a time or two. You never know what you might hear at school and regret speaking at home.

Work, that's another story. That could be where I picked up my allegedly filthy mouth. I know that I do swear occasionally. In fact, I used to be famous for one incident back when I had a real job. I was in the middle of a stressful meeting with the County Commissioners, my bosses at the time. We were talking about "funding" in terms of finding money for important environmental programs. I meant to say that we needed to find a "funding mechanism." But it came out with a different "F-word" inserted. Luckily that was before the days of televised Commissioner meetings and during the days when even some politicians had a sense of humor. These days, who the heck knows. I'd probably be starring in a viral social media video and be out of a gol darn job.

Working for the government is not where I learned bad words like the F-bomb. It was a few of those other jobs I've had over the years. Us kids were expected to work early and often. In fact, as a young man in my mid-teens, I once received a surprise back-pay check in the mail from a former employer. The note with it said that the company had been audited and it was found that they were in violation of child labor laws and owed me the enclosed money. I remember that boss due to his ethnic Norse name, not for his swearing. I also recall that he was a crabby old man and likely was even crabbier after he wrote that check.

Many other kids can say that they learned a few choice words after leaving the comfortable confines of home and the open ears of their parents. Once you get out there in the big world, working with adults, your eyes can be opened pretty wide, pretty fast, by the language assaulting your virgin ears. Some of the farmers, many of the construction workers, and most of the factory workers I labored with didn't have the same standards at home as I did.

It is likely that some of my bosses, usually men, had the most influence on my bad language. Take "Pete" for example, the head of a commercial construction crew I worked with one summer while waiting for college to resume. He had spent many long days watching over construction projects in the hot sun of places like Texas and Kansas.

I thought he was well past his prime, something a guy only twenty years old often thinks of the "Old Guy" who's supervising him. Pete would ask me and one other crew member for help with the project's blueprints. "Mike and Duncan," he'd say. "You guys have had some college. Help me figure these darn plans out. Something's not right with these freaking things."

He didn't really say it that way. I'd have a hard time working in all the four-letter words he did use. It was imaginative and influenced by all that work in the southern states where language is said to be more colorful than here Up North. As some observers used to say, "He doesn't call a spade a spade—he calls it a #%^*ing shovel!" That part of his brain hadn't been fried in the hot summer sun. At least he was always cheerful and not a crabby old man.

On the other hand, I once worked for a man

that was both a master at being crabby and using colorful language. I spent many working hours alone with "Jack" on another summer construction job. I mixed cement and hauled overloaded wheelbarrows of brick mortar while he cussed himself, his job, members of his family, and the world in general. He especially cussed me, since I always seemed to bring him mortar that was too wet or too dry or I didn't get enough cement blocks in the right places quick enough. Some of it might have been warranted. There was a day or two that I showed up a little worse for wear because I'd been up late the night before trying to figure out how to keep Jack happy and keep my much-needed job.

Jack never fired me despite these shortcomings. But he might have one day if he had noticed my reaction to one of his profane tirades. I had the job site, a big stone chimney, all prepped and was waiting high on the roof of the home. He showed up late but climbed the ladder to the roof and was in the best mood I'd ever seen. He greeted me without a bad word and started to bend over to examine the chimney flue. He stood back up, laughed, and then removed a pen and notebook from his shirt pocket. "#$%^," he said. "Don't want to lose those #$%^ing things down the #(^!@# chimney."

He then picked up his cement trowel and bent back down. The big wide-brimmed hat he always wore tumbled off his head and went straight down the bottomless black hole of the chimney.

Aaaahhh, the profanity that ensued! Indescribably profane profanity. There are not enough special characters on a keyboard to replicate it. Luckily, he had his back turned to me because I collapsed on the roof behind him. Scared for my life? Nope. I was laughing dang hard at the sight of a grown man, on a roof, waving around a cement trowel while screaming very nasty words down an innocent chimney at a lost hat. Jack's tirade went on long enough for me to get under control and back away without stepping off the roof. He stomped back down the ladder, bad words trailing behind, turning the air a vivid blue and wasn't seen for the rest of the day.

I should stress that not all the people I've worked for have had this nasty habit. There have been bosses good and bad that didn't need profanity to motivate or entertain me. However, some of the bad words from the others may have been retained and used.

So let me apologize to my mother right here and now for those bad words in the past and future. Apologies also to those cabin neighbors or visitors that might have shown up unannounced to check on me and heard a few unsavory things come from the roof while I was struggling with a crooked rafter or a jammed nail gun. Maybe even a few fishermen and fisherwomen out on the lake heard some stuff they didn't need to hear while communing with nature.

I'm sorry to you all. It seems that construction work like this cabin addition brings out the worst in me and my crappy language. Probably because I'm my own gosh darn boss on this job.

You're gol dang right I am!

And golly gee, you sure as heck had better not freakin' forget it!

A CHANGE IN POWER

A Change in Power

I was out on the cold wind-swept ice of Crooked Lake when it dawned on me that the times, they were a-changing. I had just drilled five or six holes through a foot of ice, searching for that honey hole beneath which swam a big school of golden-eyed, silver-sided crappies. Normally that would have involved firing up my old beast of a clunky, heavy gas-powered ice auger, turning the crisp northern air blue with swear words whilst yanking on the starter cord. Then continuing to sweat and swear more until the dang thing finally fired to life, blew out my sensitive old ears, and turned the swear word-laced atmosphere blue all over again with stinking two-cycle gas fumes.

Today this chore had been accomplished with minimal effort using my brand-new battery-powered ice auger. This new flashy-looking orange and black machine chewed through a foot of ice without a bad word uttered or the stink of a dead dinosaur refined into gasoline. I was cleaning the ice chips out of the holes when cabin neighbor Tom rolled up on his four-wheeler with his green and black electric auger mounted proudly in its place of honor on the front rack. He noticed my shiny new toy. Guys are like that when it comes to power tools.

"Nice auger!" he says. "How many volts is that thing?"

I swelled up a little with pride and gave him the facts—"It says one-hundred-twenty volts right there on the battery!"

I could tell right then that Tom had a bad case of auger envy. "Damn," he said. "Mine's only forty."

Take notice, all you hearty, outdoorsy Northwoods guys and gals. Change is a-comin'! We have all measured our power and worth in amounts soon to be outdated. Well-known units such as horsepower are about to become as obsolete and as useless as a horse at the Indy 500. Gasoline-powered machines, tools, and toys, the very ones we use to turn trees into firewood, to get to the other side of the lake, or to rumble through the snows of winter and the mud of spring, will soon be rusting in junkyards.

More importantly, with this transformation will come the need to find new ways of measuring our power and thus our prestige in our local communities. Things are about to get complicated because few of us are physicists who fully understand the formulas used to calculate scientific terms of power. I for one will admit that I got a "D" in the one Physics class required to graduate back in those college days. I was mighty happy to get a passing grade and move on with my life.

While we might not understand the formula

used to calculate old-school measurements like "horsepower," we do understand that 350 horsepower is adequate for our big old four-wheel-drive trucks and that 150 horsepower isn't. Furthermore, we as a community of Northwoods outdoors-types, understand that the more horsepower you have, the more power and prestige you have with what some people would call our "peers."

Move on from that ice auger. Some electric cars are now quicker, faster, and more powerful than those muscle cars we lusted over in the parking lots of our high schools. Even our big manly trucks can now be had in hybrid and electric versions. Ones that can effortlessly haul boats, campers, big loads of firewood, and even power the cabin if a storm brings an old pine tree down across a power line.

I know some guys and gals may question whether a complete change will ever happen and will fight this evolution. They do have some valid points, ones that I can nod my head about over a beverage around the campfire or at the local watering hole. For example, my power tool collection has been slowly evolving from plug-in corded tools to re-chargeable battery-powered drills, saws, and all sorts of specialty tools—or toys as some members of my family refer to them. These tools/toys are handy and portable. No need to drag a power cord around behind you that catches on ladders and corners or is too short or unplugs itself at critical moments. But the batteries and chargers needed . . .

Could some government authority or industry group come up with a standardized battery and charger system for all our tools and toys? PLEASE!!!!!

I know if you buy into one brand's advertising about being the most powerful and versatile, you can get by with one battery and charger "system." That means you have sold your power tool soul to that one company and are stuck with their "system" which will be the most expensive this year and the least powerful and versatile the next. In the meantime, you and I are stuck with a battery or two or three and a charger for every one of the many tools and toys we have piled in the garage. There the chargers and their cords mingle and tangle like a herd of garter snakes, forcing you to untangle and guess which is which.

There. I feel better now. Sorry about that tirade. Somebody had to say it.

Despite this problem and a few other ones that need to shake out over time, I believe these forces are in motion and beyond our control. The real question is how we will adapt.

How will we, as Northwoods outdoorsy types, measure our power and therefore our standing in our community? Who is leading in the race of Life? Who is "The Man" or "The Woman"—"The Person"—we look up to, compete with, and strive to be?

A Change in Power

I suggest that we take one thing at a time, forget all that competitive stuff for the moment, and work together as a community to establish our power-measuring system. This new stuff is like a foreign language to many of us. For example, based on my limited knowledge, just counting volts like Tom and I were doing with ice augers doesn't seem to be the answer. We all know that the cheap twenty-volt cordless drill we buy at a discount store to work on the cabin doesn't have the durability and power of the twenty-volt drill the professional contractor uses to fix the mistakes we created with ours. There must be more to that equation. Something maybe to do with watts, since we all know the one-hundred-watt bulb flooding the cabin yard with light burns brighter than the forty-watt bulb over the basement stairs.

There are even other less understood terms, at least by me, to consider and wonder about. Like that thing called an "amp." And what the heck is an "ohm?" So, help me out here. Think about this important topic and be ready for a serious discussion of power around the next neighborhood campfire or get together at the Buckhorn Bar.

I imagine the scientists among us may propose some kind of complicated formula like volts divided by watts multiplied by the square of pi over amps. Pardon my French but that makes me scared for our community's future and specifically mine.

I'll never really know how I stack up against my neighbors. 'Cause I never was no good at Math neither.

However, I do know someone that is good at math: our youngest son, Stevie, whom we spent a lot of college funds on. He went off to engineering school and now makes sure our beds, yes, our beds, do not cook, freeze, electrocute, or fold us in half in the dark of a cold winter's night.

Pardon me, but can I ask what the hell has happened to our world? A world where we need electrical and computer engineers like him to protect us from our "smart" beds?

Sorry about that. Spoken like a true old man. Let's see what he has to say on this subject.

"Time for the family member who was good at that dreaded 'math' subject, to step in. It can be intimidating to quantify the idea of 'power' in this transition to batteries and volts, so I'm here to tell you it is not that complicated!

"While we all like to make the Tim 'The Toolman' Taylor grunts while discussing the horsepower under the hood of our favorite pickup truck or how our snowblower has the power to send snow into our least favorite neighbor's yard, would you be excited if that number comes out bigger in this new strange electrical world?

"There are direct comparisons that can be

made between mechanical values like torque (or force), speed, and friction, and electrical ones like voltage, amps, and that weird 'ohm.' It is the same in this idea of power, whether the units of measurement are the 'horsepower' (HP) we know and love, or the misunderstood 'watt' (W). In simple terms, HP = Force x Speed. In electricity, W = Voltage x Amps. These simple equations spare you all the extra scary math and physics that play into those, but in practice 1 HP is equal to about 735 W. How's that for a big manly number?

"The only difference is that mechanical gas engines get their input values for equations in a different way than electricity does. This is also where electricity always wins out. Gas engines rely on the time it takes to rev up to output that nameplate HP value. Electricity has all the power that goes into that equation available instantaneously. While its torque or force can differ, it doesn't matter what the RPMs are, electricity is always giving you the same 'peak' value as one input of its equation.

"In the debate with Tom over one-hundred-twenty-V vs forty-V, my dad is right in the sense that his auger can work 'faster' (higher voltage can translate to more available speed), but it doesn't necessarily mean that his is more 'powerful.' That can be up to the battery's capacity. In the same vein that we know a small four-cylinder engine isn't *going to be capable of the power of a large hemi-V8, size matters here as well. A bigger battery equals more capability, because the electrical current (amps) available translates to how 'hard' something can do its work (torque or force).*

 "So, if my dad has his envy-inducing one-hundred-twenty-V auger hooked up to a two-Amp-hour capacity battery, the overall 'power' he can dish out is that volts times amps multiplication, equaling 240 watts. But if Tom's forty-V version has a ten-amp-hour battery, he can dish out four-hundred total watts. In this hypothetical scenario where all other things are equal (this is where that weird 'ohm' would come in and complicate things further than necessary in this exercise), they will both only work for one-hour total, but Tom's 'only forty' auger is going to drill more holes.

 "By this point, are you asking, 'I thought you said it's not complicated?' Well, maybe I misjudged how simple my engineering background considers these things. But if you take anything away from what I've explained, it is still that 'bigger is better.' More volts and more amps will win your hypothetical power struggle with your neighbors around that campfire or while enjoying your favorite beverages at the Buckhorn Bar.

 "While I'm here, my dad underestimates his recollection of complicated equations that his 'D' in physics achieved. That 'damn formula' for power he

suggested in jest, isn't that far from reality if you are into something like the driveshaft of your four-wheel-drive pickup truck. His formula has the torque (voltage), RPMs, or speed (amps), and even the pi (comes into play for anything rotating, as two-pi equates to one full revolution) portions of that equation pretty much figured out."

OK, Mike here. I'm back.

I don't know about you but I'm sorry I asked for that explanation or even brought this whole complicated power subject up. I got a headache and need something strong to stop my head from spinning.

How about us old guys and gals just stick to ice fishing and leave this power discussion up to the young folks to figure out?

THE EVOLUTION
OF TOOLS

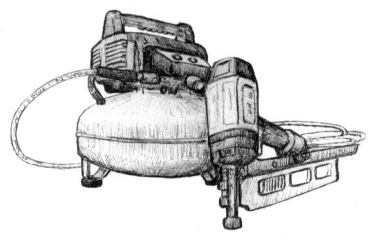

The Evolution of Tools

There's a standard prompt often used by inexperienced writers or those suffering from the dreaded curse of writers' block. It's the old trick of looking up the definition of a word in a Webster's or Funk & Wagnalls dictionary and then writing away, using the definition as the base for their work. I'm doing that here but not for those reasons since I'm an experienced writer, and although I do sometimes suffer from writers' block, that ain't the case this time.

"Tool." Look this word up in your dictionary of choice and you'll find a definition something like "a thing you hold in your hand and use to accomplish a task." So back in the day, a caveman would pick up a rock, bash open a nut or crack a small dinosaur over the noggin and proceed to have lunch. He'd used a tool, a rock in this case, to accomplish the task of eating. Or maybe he decided he was tired of life as a "caveman" and used the rock to pound a stick into the ground to hold up other sticks and eventually build a stick hut. The first real "cabin" maybe. He probably soon figured out that he needed different sizes of rocks for beating on different sizes of nuts, dinosaurs, and sticks, including maybe a big freaking rock for really

139

freaking big nuts, dinosaurs, and sticks. Things evolved. That's what we are talking about here.

When I built the original cabin, back in the day, I wasn't exactly a caveman with a rock, but I wasn't far from it. It was near the turn of the last century. The Y2K scare, if you remember that. I had a hammer, an electric circular saw with a cord, and a gas-powered generator to make the sharp teeth on the circular saw blade go around and around to zip through lumber. I pounded thousands of nails by hand through plywood sheeting and 2 x 6 lumber with that hammer, which when you think about it, is nothing more than a highly evolved rock. Over twenty years later, as I am adding an addition several sizes larger than the original cabin, I don't know how I managed it. Sure, I was over twenty years younger and maybe in better shape, but the amount of manual labor it took is inconceivable today.

Some of the tools I now have were available then, but in cruder forms and my finances had not evolved enough to consider them. That has thankfully changed. That hammer with the yellow fiberglass handle has evolved into a heavy-duty compressed-air nailer or "nail gun" as it's known in the trade. It holds about fifty nails all tied together with a paper strip. The air from an electric compressor works its magic inside the nailer and "shoots" three-inch nails through four inches of wood, with the pull of a trigger, without stopping to dig nails out of a nail pouch one by one. It will drive ten or more nails in the time it took to do one back in my caveman days and without the need to massage a sore elbow or swear at a crushed thumbnail. There's even an apple-sized "palm nailer" you hold in the palm of your hand to reach into tight spots.

The old-fashioned rock hammer also has seen less duty since I discovered the electric auto-feed screwdriver. No more bashing heavy-duty ring-shank nails through an inch of rock-hard subflooring. For this task, nails have evolved into heavy-duty screws. Feed a strip of screws into the screw gun, kneel down on the subfloor, and to the sound of "errrrt, errrrt, errrrt," the screws are in and locking down the subfloor with a minimal amount of time, labor, and cussing.

The saw? It too has evolved and been partially replaced by a shelf full of specialized cutting tools such as a "chop saw" for precise end cuts and a cordless "reciprocating saw" that is handy for fixing mistakes. Mistakes do happen when I'm in charge. That saw needs to be recharged occasionally but there's no cord to trip over or to cut off. The electrical tape on the old circular saw's power cord suggests this mishap has happened in the past. The generator is still around and has its own special storage spot in the outhouse. But we've hooked up to the electrical grid now and only need it for backup on dark and stormy nights.

There's also another type of tool that's been useful for this latest project. My relatives, friends, and neighbors. When people ask me if I am doing this project "by myself, without a contractor," my first response is something like "Yeah, but I couldn't find a general contractor that I could afford or that had time for the work."

If I am thinking clearly at the time, I'll immediately qualify that response—"but I'm getting a lot of help from relatives, friends, and neighbors."

I did much of the first floor framing myself, cutting, nailing, and screwing beams, joists, studs, and sheeting into place. Then came the task of dealing with the upper floor joists, studs, sheeting, subfloor, AND especially the roof trusses and heavy-duty, snow-load-proof roof sheeting. My back and tools were not up to those tasks even as evolved as they are. A crew of a brother, two sons, a brother-in-law, and an old college friend somehow converged on the site to help with that. I rented this magically evolved ladder type thing called an "electric man-lift" and the second floor appeared with walls and trusses all in place, just waiting for the roof sheeting.

You might say these guys did not fit the classic definition of tools since I wasn't holding them in my hand. Whatever—I had certainly "used" them to accomplish a task.

Unfortunately, they all had lives of their own and had to get back to jobs and families before the roof was sheeted, leaving the bare open roof trusses exposed to the long, snowy, cold winter that was bearing down on the project. I picked away at the sheeting for several more weeks with the help of a son or two here and there. The weather didn't cooperate much. Twice, maybe three times, the second-floor loft had to be shoveled clear of six or seven or eight inches of snow that floated down through the roof trusses to the expensive non-waterproof subflooring. Shoveling snow was back-breaking, time-consuming manual labor that did not move the project forward and made scrambling around on the steep pitch of the second story even more daunting for a lone, aging writer-turned-carpenter.

This brought back a few memories from the original cabin construction project some twenty years ago. The shingle-less cabin had already survived the storm of the century, the famous Fourth-of-July mega-storm that rolled through the cabin site and then moved on to flatten thousands of acres of stately pine trees in the Boundary Waters Canoe Area Wilderness.

Brother-in-law Darv and I were scurrying around on the roof, nailing down shingles, trying to get the roof water-tight before more thunderstorms heated up. My seventy-year-old dad was convinced he should be out on that steep-pitched slippery roof with us. I forbade him to step foot on it, convinced an ambulance would be needed at a time and place where cell phones and cell phone coverage were not available. He perched on the top rung of a shaky ladder, scowling and chirping at us like an angry squirrel who has been banned from the bird feeder.

"Stay where you are, don't even think about it, Old Man!"

I can remember yelling that at him, not being kind or diplomatic. Just trying to force him back down to the ground where he belonged. Now here I was, over twenty years later, having evolved to the age of almost seventy, trying to lift heavy sheets of plywood up to and onto a steep roof, two stories in the air. Then a couple of new tools came to my rescue.

I was hanging out with neighbors Tom and Marv on a Sunday evening, resting my aching muscles from a weekend of work with son Andy. We had nailed down a few panels of the roof sheeting. Not enough sheets though, given that another major winter storm was bearing down on the North Country, forecast to bury my unfinished project in a foot or more of new snow, with added wind and cold. I must have cried in my beer too much about the unfinished work. Or it's possible these two guys conspired amongst themselves prior to our evening get-together. They cut my complaining and moaning short. "We're both showing up at 8:30 tomorrow morning. Put us to work."

The Evolution of Tools

I had doubts about the wisdom of their offer. We had all evolved, so to speak, if you count the bodily changes and damages of the aging process as "evolution." But they followed through on their words the next morning and I had to use them. The average age of this three-person roofing crew was around seventy, give or take, maybe even a little older if you're better with math than I am. You might say we were not just evolved. We were "highly evolved"!

Tom ordered me to drag that fancy air nailer up into the rafters and stay there. He and Marv cut sheets of plywood to the proper length and maneuvered them up through the roof trusses while I fed the nail gun more nails and tried to keep up. As a measure of their skills, I only had to lower one sheet back down due to a longer-than-needed cut.

The last nail was shot from the gun about six hours later. Six hours of continuous work. Those guys didn't even allow me a union-required coffee break or lunch hour. It left me exhausted with muscle aches in places I had forgotten that muscles existed. However, we all survived and the roof sheeting was on, protecting the addition from the blizzard that did occur over the next several days.

It left me so relieved, so happy, and so grateful that I cried. Yes, I did. Real tears. I'm not the least bit ashamed to write that down and admit it. In fact, if I was using an old-fashioned typewriter, there would be tear stains on the typewriter paper right now.

One of the crazy things about the English language is how one word can have many meanings or perhaps a formal meaning and a slang meaning. You might say that words, like tools, can evolve. Go back to the dictionaries again. This time check the slang section. A tool can be defined as the useful hand-held object we discussed earlier. Or it can be a derogatory slang term to describe "a person, usually a male, that is foolish and may be prone to manipulation or being used by other people smarter than him."

Thus, some readers wonder why I would call relatives, friends, and neighbors "tools" and not clarify that I'm referring to them as being used to accomplish building tasks like holding up sheeting and cutting lumber and plywood. It's likely that their friends and loved ones have thought that they were being used and manipulated by someone—me in this case. After all, many of them have their own cabins, don't need to use mine, and don't get much of a reward for their work except maybe some free pizza and the gift of a cheap bottle of booze.

Maybe so. But I am a "non-fiction" writer, not one of those liars who calls himself a "fiction" writer. So, trust me on this one, when I salute these guys and call them "one hell of a bunch of tools," I mean it as a good thing.

SNOW

Snow

I was hoping that the leaves of the tall aspens and oaks towering over the cabin site would be the biggest natural annoyance of the construction project. They drifted down from above, landing on the unprotected floor of the new addition, creating a new mosaic artwork every morning. A collage of natural, free-range, organic art, glistening with morning dew, laid down in random patterns of shining gold, bright orange, and rusted red. I tried to appreciate each morning's new masterpiece, but every morning started with the task of destroying these masterpieces, sweeping, shoveling, and blowing yesterday's leaves from first the cement of the basement, then the subflooring of the first floor, and finally from the high airy floor of the loft. I soon grew tired of this daily routine.

Then came the snow. I never had to shovel snow out of the basement. However, every morning seemed to begin with the manual labor of shoveling, sweeping, and blowing the white fluffy stuff or the hard crunchy, melted, frozen stuff out of the loft as I struggled to sheet the roof and enclose the upper level. That was just what fell on the limited area of the construction project. Also needing to be dealt with were feet of the same stuff that fell on the driveway, the yard, and the piles of construction materials stacked and awaiting use.

I had hoped for a relatively snow-free winter like sometimes happens. Nope. I got historic amounts of snow. Historic at least since us newcomers to this part of the world started keeping records.

I'm not sure that the native peoples before us kept records or told tall tales about tough winters and horrible snow depths. I did a little research and came up with nothing from the usual "reliable" sources. This research did turn up a few interesting diversions that sent me down multiple internet rabbit holes. It was a good way to kill time on a cold, dark, and snowy night in the middle of another record-setting blizzard. The weather guy on the local channel had predicted that four or five, or six to eight, or maybe even eight to twelve more inches of snow might be dropping from the skies, settling like a suffocating white blanket over the construction project, the stacked materials, the yard, and the driveway.

I fired up the smart phone and started the research, beginning with one of those urban myth type sayings that claim that the Inuit people of the Arctic Circle region have unique words for over a hundred types of snow. Instead of calling it light, fluffy snow, they might call it just one unique word. Hard, sleety snow might have another one-word name, much like languages that use a single written character for each word instead of multiple letters that make up words in various combinations.

Here's the urban myth part. There is a controversial theory with a big, long name —"linguistic-relativity hypothesis" or "Whorfianism," named after a so-called expert with the last name of "Whorf." Other "experts" of the language argue that the "experts" in the many-unique-words camp, simply don't understand how the Inuit language works. It's complicated, but these linguistic geniuses say the Arctic natives just use adjectives different than the English language and not every slightly different color or texture of snow has its own name.

Missing in this whole argument seems to be the opinion of the native people themselves. I can't help but picture them sitting on the sidelines of the debate, in their warm clothes, holding their preferred adult beverages, and laughing at the arguments thrown around by "experts." After all, these hardy people must have a huge sense of humor. Who could survive living in eight or nine months of snow for thousands of years without a good sense of humor?

This thought sent me off down those internet rabbit holes, researching deeper as the wind howled and more snow fell around the cabin. What words for "snow" do other languages common to the history of the North Country have?

The area around our cabin has been host to many different groups of native peoples over the ten-thousand years or so since the last glacier melted back into Canada, allowing plants, animals, and people to return. The most recent are the Anishinaabe, also known as the Ojibwe. Their word for snow is "goon," pronounced pretty much like what you would call some big brutish guy or what a hockey fan would call a player who's noted for picking fights. That seems ironic in this most hockey-fanatic place in the world.

The next people to appear in this part of the country were likely French Canadian fur traders back four or five hundred years. They often over-wintered with the native peoples and thus had plenty of experience with snow. "La neige" appears to be the word used for snow, pronounced in a husky, sexy way by the lady on the internet site I visited—"laa nayge." This goes against the one-word theory of the Arctic languages and even English. Apparently the French like to use multiple words or syllables when some of us think one will do.

Then in the last two centuries came a mixed wave of other European settlers bound and determined to tame this wild land by logging forests and grubbing up fields to plant crops. My blood relatives were part of this influx. Genetic testing has proven my background to be mainly Scandinavian and other northern European types. Family history says I'm at least half Norwegian. Those folks call snow "sno." That internet lady pronounces it as a short nasal "snaa." This seems strange since every other word in the Norwegian language seems to be long and drawn out, especially those words with an "o." Maybe that's just us talking Minnesooooootan.

Iceland, the only Scandinavian country which I have visited, uses an old form of the Norse language. There snow is "snjor." Which figures. Icelanders seem to find a way to put a "j" or a "k" and especially an "s," into just about every word in their language. It's pronounced "snee-yor" or something like that. It gets more complex from there since there's plenty of snow in Iceland. Some experts of this language claim there's over a hundred words for snow in the Icelandic dialect. That sounds familiar . . .

"Drifting snow" is "skafrenningur." There's the "k" instead of the "j" this time and I'm not even going to try to pronounce this word. Things get even more complicated from here. Take "fukt" for example. It means a "very small amount of snow." I'm afraid to try to pronounce that one. It looks and probably sounds like an "F-word" I shouldn't be saying in public.

"Fukt" looks to me like a word used for a whole lot of snow that falls at an inopportune time. Something I might have used multiple times this winter. Something even a usually sane, non-cussing person might use early and often while once again shoveling out a construction project. A too-often repeated task that results in colorful adjectives added to the word "snow" in whatever language you speak.

DAD'S TACKLE BOX

Dad's Tackle Box

As the oldest son in a family of five kids, I naturally inherited responsibilities that came with that position. Responsibilities like mandatory arguments with Dad about how late a teenaged boy could stay out on a Friday night. Or Saturday morning. Pushing the limits on what kind of music was acceptable to bring home from college for the summer. Discussions with Dad about how long the hair of a small-town businessman's son could be without rumors and whispers starting at the coffee shop. Fighting an epic battle about having a car at college and what sort of car that would be.

Those early conflicts gave way to a mostly peaceful understanding between two adults and the mutual recognition that we had things in common. A common sense of adventure and a love of fishing helped mend those fences.

Dad had more time for adventure and fishing once he made the transition from the tractors and the cows of a dairy farmer seven days and nights a week, to the office and computers of a hard-working insurance agent. That change allowed him to take the family on epic road trip vacations that included adventure and fishing. Fishing for crappies, trout, northern pike, and walleyes in northern Minnesota.

159

The Last Cabin

Salmon and crabs off the rocky shores of Oregon, where waves crashed over us and threatened to drag a couple dumb Minnesotans out to the Pacific Ocean. A western camping trip that included a stop at Grand Tetons National Park.

The crowded campground at that national park didn't provide enough adventure for him. He found a trail headed off through the forest towards the mountains and the Snake River. My two younger brothers and I followed him into the wilderness without question. No bear spray? No problem. It probably hadn't been invented yet anyway. The four of us tried to be noisy, talking loudly and maybe even singing, to scare away bears and other large beasts. We did a poor job of it. In the middle of a sunny opening in the piney forest, a herd of sleeping elk was surprised to find us stumbling through them. They leaped up, cows snorting warning calls, calves squealing in fright, and thundering past close enough to touch and smell. It's lucky they weren't bears.

Shortly after that encounter we stepped out of the forest and onto the banks of the Snake River. The Grand Tetons themselves towered in the background, lit in the sun in all their snowcapped mountainous glory. The Snake River tumbled down a rocky bed, past forested banks shimmering in the sunlight. Then the elk showed themselves again. They splashed across the river, buckskin brown against the forest and mountain backdrop, a scene straight out of a staged TV commercial.

Then came the fishing. I had spent hard-earned vacation dollars on a fishing license. Those dollars had been wasted up until this point. The trout at the crystal-clear campground lake had cruised past, taunting me, and refusing to bite. I carried an old-fashioned Minnesota northern/walleye fishing rod and a few lures along on this hike, just in case river fish had a different attitude. On my first cast into the waters of Wyoming's Snake River, a trout was fooled by my Minnesota lake lure. I fought it to the riverbank and flopped it out onto shore. There lay one of the prettiest fish in the mountains, a big wild Cutthroat trout, with gold and rainbow-colored flanks and the characteristic crimson-red slash along the bottom of the jaw. I was in heaven and knew it for certain when I caught another on the second cast.

I was fifteen when this happened, thankful that I was on an adventure with Dad and oblivious to the strife and turmoil that would change our relationship in just a few years.

Now that Dad had left us after ninety-one years of a full and eventful life, I was tasked by my mother with another responsibility. Since I was the oldest son and Dad's main fishing partner, I was to sort through his fishing tackle box and distribute any usable contents to worthy sons and daughters, grandsons and granddaughters, great-grandsons and great-granddaughters, and perhaps even a few great-

great-grandsons and great-great-granddaughters.

I waited over a year to tackle that job. On a cold March evening at the cabin, all by myself, I mixed some brandy with a little ice, then sat down and opened the tackle box.

Lest you think I was anticipating opening a relic of a metal tackle box full of antique lures worth many dollars, think again. My dad's early years were spent in small-town Iowa and rural Minnesota. There wasn't much money for fancy fishing tackle. What little did exist went up in flames along with a tractor and tools in a machine shed fire on our last farm.

Having fished with him and this replacement tackle box, I knew what to expect and that's what I found. Inside the two-tone green, hip-roofed box was a generic mix of gear. The top trays held loose lead split-shot sinkers and small hooks. The things you'd use with worms or minnows for panfish. Also well represented were a bunch of red and white feathered crappie jigs and a few old-fashioned round bobbers of the same colors.

Tucked into the lower shelves were a dozen or so minnow-shaped lures with treble hooks, the kind you troll along the weed lines of Minnesota lakes, hoping to catch a walleye or northern pike. In this case, mainly northerns since those and crappies were his favorite fish. Many of these were in pristine condition, still in their original boxes. I recognized some as gifts I had given him for birthdays and

Father's Day. I understood why they still shined from unopened boxes. He was afraid to lose such pretty and expensive gifts to the likes of toothy, line-cutting northern pike or sharp-edged rocks.

Except for those treasures, most of the tackle was well-used and outdated, not suitable for passing on to the younger generations, at least if they were serious about catching fish. I set aside the newer ones, determined to slowly meter them out as I fished with my sons, my nephews and nieces, and all those others. Two others did stand out as worthy of special treatment.

A red and white treble-hooked spoon, the famous "Daredevil" brand, will go to my tackle box. Some of my earliest memories of fishing involve chilly mornings trolling the shores of Minnesota lakes with Dad and his friend Denny, dragging one of these red and white spoons on my thick black braided fishing line, hoping and praying that a northern pike would ambush the lure and bend my prized blue fiberglass fishing rod.

The other lure was a classic example of what manufacturers convince fishermen to buy as the next great monster-catching artificial bait. It was an oblong-shaped lure, roughly minnow-like, made of hard plastic, painted a strange purple background with white spots. It was not an elegant work of fishing tackle art, more likely to scare a fish than entice one to strike. Attached to the front was a heavy metal leader to ensure any toothy fish that was fooled by the ugly thing would not bite through the line and steal it away to the watery depths. The leader also likely robbed the lure of any lifelike action, making it doubly safe from loss.

It will go in my tackle box alongside the red and white spoon. I'm thinking that my sons and I, and their mother and their wives, will have a new competition out on the pontoon boat when trolling the shores of Crooked Lake. Should the fishing be too easy, or a fisherperson be too cocky, that lure will be a challenge. "Catch a fish on Grandpa's Ugly Lure. I bet you a beer you can't."

Finally, the bottom of the tackle box needed attention. I pulled out a tangled mass of kinked and twisted line, all rolled up and knotted together. A sinker and a crappie jig were attached at one end. At the other was an old push-button spin-casting reel, a simple piece of equipment that many fishermen begin and end their careers with.

The mess spoke of a frustrating incident somewhere on an unknown lake, where the tangle became such a problem that the reel, line, and lure were removed from a rod and shoved into the bottom of the tackle box to be dealt with later. Here I was, dealing with it.

I cut off most of the line and scrapped it. I saved a knotted tangle that included the sinker, lure, and the worthless old reel. They'll have a place of honor on the fireplace mantle at the cabin. A little reminder of the past, of lives and fishing, all messy and tangled together.

THE GREAT THAW

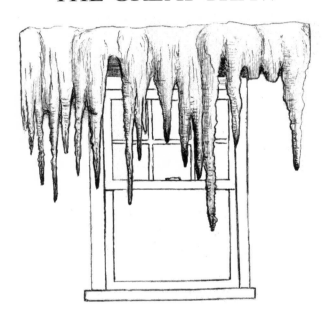

As much as winter seemed to last forever, there did come a time when the mountains of snow piled around the cabin and drifted on the roof started to succumb to the warming rays of the sun. I welcomed the sun after a cold, dark, and snowy winter. With the change in seasons came a new challenge. All the melting snow was turning liquid. This liquid found its way through the unfinished addition's roof, dripping down into the unfinished living space below.

The roof was covered in sturdy 5/8-inch sheeting, some of the best money can buy. It might look tight and waterproof from a distance. Look closer and there were small gaps between each sheet. Gaps mandated by manufacturer's specs and building codes to allow for minor expansion and contraction. By my calculations there were over two-hundred feet of gaps. Two-hundred feet of gaps leaking melted snow down into the addition to flow across the expensive non-weatherproof subflooring and pool in the basement.

I would have liked to get a tarp or some tar paper on the roof last fall before it snowed on that leaking sheeting. That wasn't possible due to another nasty blizzard that showed itself about a minute after the last sheet was nailed down. I had to get creative and deal with that mess now.

The first line of defense was plastic sheeting and tarps laid across the floors to catch the minor drips at the beginning of the thaw. The water pooled on the plastic and then froze overnight when temperatures dropped below freezing in the unheated, uninsulated upper floor. Each morning, I climbed a ladder into the loft and scraped ice from the tarps with a metal dustpan, dropped the stiff water into a bucket, and dumped the bucket out an open window. I thought that was kinda genius. I was working with the weather for once instead of against it.

The melt increased as the temps rose and new snow from new blizzards piled on the remains of the last blizzard. The floor tarp strategy wasn't enough once it stayed above freezing after dark and the melt continued all night. Now I was climbing into the loft several times a day with the shop vac to suck liquid water off the tarps and dump it out a window. This had limitations as the volume increased and endangered the expensive tools and building materials stored below in the first floor.

Then came the bucket brigade. I searched the cabin and storage sheds for every kind of water-holding container that could be found. A garbage can was placed underneath the drip in the future bathroom. Two ice fishing buckets and a minnow bucket attempted to contain drips in the future bedroom. A couple of household waste baskets and a kitchen dish tub served the same duty in the will-be living room. The drips kept multiplying faster than my inventory of containers. The final act of desperation was pressing into duty the camping porta potty under a new drip in the kitchen. That added an aroma that shouldn't be found in any kitchen.

More buckets weren't the answer to the problem. There was still snow packed on the roof waiting for its turn to shine in the sun and yet another dang blizzard of wet heavy snow was bearing down on the Northwoods. This one was forecast to drop another foot of problem white stuff on the roof, to melt, to drip in the loft, and make its way to the buckets, wastebaskets, and porta potty down below.

Maybe I could find a way to cover the existing roof snow so at least the new stuff would melt off elsewhere. I hunted up two big tarps. All I needed was a way to get them spread over the two-story roof to protect it. I dug into my bag of tricks.

To be honest, neighbor Tom suggested this hack during a late-night winter strategy session. He had been watching construction videos too. I tied a long rope through the hole in the end of the handle of a big freakin' adjustable wrench, twirled it a few times, and sent the wrench with the rope trailing flying high in the air, over the top of the snow-covered leaking roof.

I didn't accomplish this on the first attempt.

The Last Cabin

There's a new dent in the log siding of the old part of the cabin, right below a big glass window. That near miss was almost an expensive learning experience. I also moved my truck to a safer place after another errant throw and I noticed the dog moved off to a respectable distance, not inclined to play fetch with this dangerous contraption. I finally got the rope up and over the roof and down to the other side. I repeated the same with another rope, and a few more tosses, and then used the ropes to pull a tarp up and over the roof.

I'd still have to deal with the melt water from the old snow covered by the tarp. However, the tarp should ensure that the snow from the upcoming blizzard would either slide or melt off without dripping down into my buckets.

One of the challenges in this exercise was what color of tarp to use. I had at my disposal two reversible tarps. One was blue on one side and silver on the other. The second was green and brown. I decided on the green and brown, and, after some careful consideration, went green side up. This may sound like a trivial thing given the circumstances, but in projects like this you face a lot of critics and have to answer many questions about materials and color selections. I was hoping for spring to come soon so I went with matching green. Agreed?

If spring ever showed its face, the next challenge would be rain. Lots of rain if the current precipitation pattern continued. April showers bring

May flowers—and wet sheeting on the unprotected exterior walls of the addition. It was time to resort to a little "Northwoods siding" to cover and protect those walls.

I'm certain that some readers already know where I'm going. For those less-informed souls, let me explain. There is a construction product that is generically called "house wrap." It's the white plastic fabric you see covering the sides of houses under construction in suburban sub-divisions. House wrap's main purpose is to seal the exterior of a house from drafts and moisture. Some type of permanent siding is usually applied over it within a matter of days. However, in the Northwoods or other rural areas, you often see house wrap covering the walls of both old and new construction for years at a time. It is the new 21st century version of tar paper, as in the "tar paper shacks" people used to refer to.

I happened to have a couple rolls in stock and had the help of my two sons. We rolled and stapled it over the walls and soon had the addition waterproofed against spring rains. That was an easy job compared to the wrench-throwing tarp-pulling for the roof. It also came with designer questions.

The house wrap was the standard bright white with big bold blue letters advertising the man-ufacturer. I would have preferred to start rolling it from the southwest corner of the cabin. That would have put the seams between the two rolls at a corner and made more efficient tidy use of this expensive stuff. That would have put the letters upside down and hard to read or showing through the fabric from the side against the wall. This would have again raised questions about my fashion sense. So, we rolled from the southeast corner and overlapped the ends in the middle of a wall. Note that if anyone complains about this seam or the wrinkles in the plastic, I will kindly invite them to show up and help next time.

As we rolled and stapled the bland white plastic to the walls, it occurred to me that people with more fashion sense, and the manufacturers of house wrap, are missing a marketing opportunity. I know house wrap is not supposed to be used as long-term siding. Realistically, it obviously is used this way in many locales. So why not go with the flow and print some up in other colors and maybe with designs? Something like the old "depression brick" tar paper that used to cover the classier tar paper shacks, or maybe even rustic wood-grain or log patterns.

I might not use it since I'm planning on some high-class siding in the near future. Then again who knows? If it keeps snowing and raining like the past six months, I might have white Northwoods siding with big blue letters showing for a long time.

CRAP HAPPENS

Crap Happens

Moms and grandmothers often share sound bits of wisdom learned from fruitful lives. One of my favorites is "bad things always happen in threes." Bad things like the untimely demise of celebrities or relatives. One goes, two more follow in quick succession. The more blunt ones might also say that "crap happens," or something like that. I'm here to tell you that they are right, and it doesn't always involve dying.

Let me tell you about my recent misfortunes, with a little dramatic effect added to make things more interesting. Things that will make my mom cringe when she reads this because she's been regularly cautioning me to "be careful" as I proceed with the cabin construction process.

The first did have something to do with the cabin construction, and had a witness. I can't get too carried away with embellishments. But I'll do my best.

There I was, high in the rafters of the second story of the cabin addition, about to make some minor adjustment that could be done without son Andy holding the ladder. Picture me twenty feet off the ground, on the top rung of the ladder, when the feet of the ladder slide backwards and send me tumbling down.

While most of those "facts" are technically

true, the ladder was perched on the second floor of the addition, and I had just started up the ladder. Thus, the fall from those lofty rafters to the hard wood was only around five feet. Still, my elbow and hip did not take kindly to that five feet. As you've probably heard before, falling is easy and painless whether it's five feet or five thousand feet. The landing part is what gets hard and painful.

I lay on the cold hard floor for a minute or two, doing an inventory of working body parts while Andy hovered over me, and his mother yelled up to ask what all the noise was about. I was lucky this time. The paramedic checked my bodily functions, and I went back to work with that elbow and hip complaining but still intact. Just to be honest, the paramedic was daughter-in-law Steph who was already on the scene, didn't have far to travel, and has dealt with worse cases over the course of her career.

I waited a few months for the next adventure in injury. Both sons and a whole bunch of nephews and great nephews and nieces were scheduled to show up at the cabin. I took a break from dangerous construction activities and involved them in the fun of splitting firewood with the new log splitter. What could go wrong operating a piece of equipment capable of splitting two-foot-wide logs into kindling?

Things were going well to begin with. Then my middle finger of my left hand, the finger you might wave in some fit of road rage, got in the way of the log splitter and a log. Picture a hand in the wrong place. The middle finger in the wrong place. The log splitter's steel jaws closing in on that finger with the manufacturer's stated specification of twenty-seven tons of hydraulic force.

I'm happy to report that isn't a true picture of the situation. I still have that finger even if it is still painful after several months. Truth be told, I was lifting a log into place to demonstrate the operation of that beastly machine when the log slipped from my clumsy grasp and fell, crushing that middle finger between the log and the hard iron frame of the splitter. No amputation was involved although I did consider that procedure to rid myself of a very painful black and blue fingernail. Luckily the paramedic took care of that with a hot needle, burning a hole through the nail and releasing the pressure. The same paramedic just happened to be on site, just like the ladder fall.

So now we are getting down to the third bad thing happening, to validate what those moms and grandmoms say about series of threes.

Let's play with a little more dramatic effect and view this instance from the eyes of an unsuspecting neighbor who arrives on-scene after all the happenings. Kinda like one of those TV shows where investigators try to piece together what happened at a crime scene after the fact.

Neighbor Tom walks over to the cabin to

check on progress. He's been off in the woods playing with chainsaws along with our other neighbor Marv. They heard ambulance sirens in the vicinity, and he wonders if I know what was going on.

He finds that I am not on the scene, swinging a hammer and swearing as usual. Nobody's home even though my truck is still parked in the usual spot and Sage, the construction supervisor and ball retriever, is shut in the cabin. He walks down to the lake. The unoccupied pontoon is still tied to the dock. He walks back to the cabin and investigates deeper. Over by the big boulder that protects the cabin's well, he finds a stained T-shirt and one sock that used to be white. The sock is now colored red, bright red, with what he deduces, since he's a smart guy, to be somebody's blood. Lots of somebody's bright red blood.

Intrigued, he investigates further. Back towards the outhouse he finds a brush cutter, a gas-powered weed whacker with a saw blade on the front instead of string. The kind we call a "zinger" because you rev the engine, let the saw blade gain the momentum of thousands of revolutions per second and then bump it against small trees. "ZING." The tree falls over, amputated from its stump.

Now he starts to put one and one and one together and comes up with three. Yet there's more clues to this Northwoods mystery. The door of the outhouse swings open in the breeze. Right next to the door, a steel fence post has been thrust through the wall of the adjacent storage shed, tearing a long gash downward through its plastic fabric covering . . .

Curiosity piqued, he decides to give me a call. I happened to have my cell phone handy when he called and could answer because I was playing the waiting game between X-rays and stitches at the local hospital's emergency room. He was able to call Marv after the call and give a report. "Those sirens? It was Mike. We have to drive into town and pick him up at the hospital."

Like most of life's happenings, the real story was crappy, but less dramatic than the one Tom had pieced together. "No," I related to him. "I didn't fire up the brush cutter, the Zinger, and proceed to amputate my foot. I was taking the Zinger out of the outhouse when I stumbled over the rusty steel fence post being used to prop the door open. That rusty steel fence post has a rusty steel pointy metal flange sticking out of it to grab and hold better in the dirt. In this case, that sharp rusty pointy flange buried itself deep in my clumsy leg and ripped open a good-sized gash, further resulting in the Zinger flying off to the side and the fence post impaling the storage shed."

This rapid series of events had forced me to start swearing and hobble over to the rock by the well to assess the damage. I expected to find a bruised, scraped, very painful shinbone. The type of thing you see after walking into the trailer hitch sticking out of the back of a truck. I pulled up my pants leg and didn't like what I saw. Blood. Lots of blood-red blood. Blood-red blood gushing from a long deep gash alongside my scraped and bruised shinbone.

Since Tom and Marv were far away playing with chainsaws, since my own personal paramedic was not on site this time, and since Sage just wanted to play with her ball, I was forced to make that dreaded 911 call. All one-handed while trying to stop the gushing blood-red blood with my other hand, my dirty old T-shirt, and a white sock.

The nice people of the ambulance crew and emergency room staff patched me together. They "numbed the crap out of it" (technical medical term that they used) and stopped the bleeding with only a dozen stitches and a few big Band-Aids. They even found I had a broken ankle. Or at least had one in the past. "The X-rays say it's all healed, so don't worry about it."

So, I've had my run of bad luck and survived the dreaded three bad things moms and grandmoms warn us about. Hopefully I'm good for a while, although I don't know how long the period between the threes is. I also learned a lesson regarding other wisdom they might pass on. Remember that line about wearing clean clothes and underwear just in case bad things happen and you must go to the hospital where people learn that you are filthy and uncouth and maybe have a mother or grandmother that doesn't care?

Picture me sitting on a landscaping rock in the

hospital parking lot, waiting for my ride back to the cabin, unhappy with my present situation. A nice lady drove past, then stopped, backed up, and rolled down her window. "Sir," she asked quietly. "Do you need help?"

"No," I replied. "I'm fine"

"Are you sure?" she asked. "I'd give you a ride anywhere."

"No, no," I said quickly, waving my cell phone. "I've got friends coming to get me."

"OK," she said before driving away. "But I'll help if you need anything."

Yeah, there I was. Long greasy gray hair and an untrimmed beard neglected for weeks due to construction schedules. I'm wearing torn pants smeared with a weeks' worth of construction grime and dog slobber, no T-shirt, one sock, and a sweatshirt that belonged in the dump. Let's not even mention the underwear . . .

QUESTIONS

Questions

I don't remember people asking many questions about constructing my first cabin some twenty-five years ago. Maybe it was more acceptable back in that day to do stuff yourself. Maybe I was clear that it was just a small rustic cabin in the woods, something like Henry David Thoreau built with about fifteen dollars, some used nails and boards, and a few borrowed tools. Then again, I was twenty-five years younger. I was still less than half a century old and so were most of my friends. So maybe they didn't think it was a big deal.

These days, on this new and much bigger project, those same friends are full of questions. I must admit to egging them on by posting construction updates on social media, which wasn't available back in those good old days. Now both true friends and electronic friends can drive me crazy with questions about my progress, my abilities, and, of course, my sanity.

The questions started with the most obvious. Them: "Can't you just hire somebody, a general contractor, that will actually get the project done?"

This one has a few easy answers that most people seem to understand. Me: "The good contractors around here are busy. And they are mostly building lake 'cabins' for people who are living some form of the lifestyle of the rich and famous. Their so-called cabins will be big enough and fancy enough to be featured in *Better Log Homes and Gardens* or something like that. They haven't got time for this project, or they want to turn it into a bigger, more expensive one. One guy wanted $350,000 to build me an addition twice as big as my house!"

Most nod their heads at that and relate the myths they have heard from others: "Yeah, and I hear the contractors around here would rather hunt and fish than work anyway."

Other questions aren't so easily answered. Them: "Why didn't you go with a full basement instead of a four-foot head-knocking crawl space?" "How come you didn't build up from a cement slab on-grade and build the heating system into the floor like my neighbor did?"

For these experts, I must go deeper in detail and explain things like topography, physics, high water tables, and the cost of dealing with these issues. Things like engineers, their engineering calculations, engineered plans, and engineer costs. This usually shuts them up. Engineers scare people and everybody knows they are expensive.

Then come the questions about space utilization. Them: "What are you going to do in the old cabin space?" "What's going to be up in the loft?"

Questions

Me: "The old cabin space has a nice view of the lake and will likely be a family room with some kind of sleeping arrangement—like a sofa bed."

The loft space questions are easier to answer. Me: "I've told the kids that the loft space is their problem. They can do whatever they want with it. And pay for it."

There are other questions that are harder to answer, especially on the day when you get all the building-related permits in hand and folks seem to think the work will start that day or the very next day.

Them: "When is the electrician going to move the power line so you can get the foundation started?"

Them: "When is the cement guy going to show up so you can get a floor down and the walls up?"

Them: "When is the sewer system guy going to show up so you can get rid of the outhouse?"

Them: "Has the sewer guy showed up yet?"

Them: "Has the sewer guy called you yet?"

The easy answer to all of these is the same. Me: "Whenever he shows up. How about I let you know when he does?"

But this sometimes doesn't stop the questions. Them: "Why don't you just hire someone else, someone that will show up?"

That question is a tough one and I must get more in-depth with the answer. Me: "I've checked all these guys out with my friends and contacts in the construction business. They are recommended for both quality and reasonable prices. I have hired the best and contrary to those myths you've heard, the good ones are busy. What would the other guys be like?"

That usually gets them thinking and bobbing their heads in reluctant agreement. Then they ask the same questions the very next day.

This problem is probably due to the fact that most of my friends, like me, aren't getting any younger. Some of the repeated questions have something to do with fading memories, including mine. That's why we are friends and can tell the same stories every time we get together. Because we can't remember what we talked about the last time.

There have been many other questions, questioning finer design-related details. Them: "Why isn't there a door on this side?" "Why is the kitchen here?" Even "Where's the new campfire pit going to be?"

And there is the question that comes up time and time again. Them: "Aren't you getting kinda old to be climbing around on ladders and roofs, building a cabin?"

Finally, we have a valid repeat question, one that deserves an honest answer.

I remember building the first humble cabin. My dad helped me with the initial stages, placing rebar in cement forms, handing tools off to me and the like. I drew the line when it came to the walls, roof, and things like climbing ladders. I told him he had to start acting his age.

I remember that story because here I am, twenty-five years later, the same age as he was, climbing around on roofs and ladders, trying not to slip, fall, or slide down the steep roof and glide off into the wild blue yonder like a flying squirrel launching from a bird feeder. I guess that is the definition of irony.

Which brings up my answer to the question of being too old for major construction projects. I'd like to retort something classic like, "Hell no, seventy is the new forty-five!" The truth is, as long days, and longer days, add up to months of hard work, I just don't know. Today I feel like I'm eighty-five.

I'm not done building things just yet. I might take on new projects like a storage shed or garage in the future. But I'm pretty damn sure this will be the last cabin.

Made in the USA
Middletown, DE
25 August 2024